I0575521

Six Months of Forever

Lyss Agri

Eula Rae Printing & Publishing

Published by Eula Rae Printing & Publishing™
Rockland County, New York
www.eularae.com

ISBN (Paperback): 979-8-9993901-0-3
ISBN (eBook): 978-0-9976748-8-0

Cover design: Lyss Agri / Eula Rae Printing & Publishing
Interior design & formatting: Eula Rae Printing & Publishing

Printed in the United States of America.
First Edition: 2026

Contents

About the Author

{ Forever, Almost }

Silence.

Funny, isn't it?

How it isn't empty at all. How it presses in, louder than any scream could. You know the silence I mean. The one that follows after you've dared to speak; after you've bared some fragile, inconvenient part of yourself, only to be met with nothing. No reply. Just the dull confirmation that you've been seen. That's the word, isn't it?

Seen.

Not acknowledged. Not cared for. Left open like a wound, like a message with a blinking cursor mocking you.

It's not silence. It's erasure. You feel it pounding in your chest because invisibility is its own kind of violence.

And this is the world we live in now: scrolling, swiping, buzzing. A million voices colliding at once. All that noise, and still, somehow, you're alone—crowded by faces, drowned in performance, starved of connection.

But there's something heroic about those who still try. The ones who keep reaching, keep writing, keep pressing send even when the only thing they get in return is silence.

People like you.

Overthinkers. Overfeelers. The ones who replay every moment, cut it into pieces, and hold it up to the light like glass. You are not invisible. Not to me.

And then there was me.

Not living. Not really. Not thriving. Not even trying.

Just...existing. Going through the motions. Filling the space with distractions so I didn't have to hear the emptiness rattling inside my chest. Breathing, but not alive.

Love?

Don't make me laugh. Love was locked away, stored in the attic with the other broken things. It belonged to some past version of myself—some naive fool who hadn't yet learned what silence tastes like.

But life has claws. It slips in where you least expect. One moment you're numb. The next, something cracks. A spark. A whisper. An almost. You feel it before you admit it: change.

{ Before Her }

I DIDN'T THINK I was lost. Not really. I had a job. I had friends—or at least people I could text when I needed to pretend I wasn't rotting inside. I had the smile, the laugh, the mask. I wore it so well I almost believed it. Almost.

But I wasn't living. I was drifting. A ghost in my own body. Days looping on repeat, hours folding into each other until time didn't matter. A soft kind of suffocation.

And the silence.

Always the silence. Every unanswered message felt like a verdict: too much, not enough, irrelevant. So I stopped asking. Stopped hoping. Built walls so high even I couldn't climb them.

Until you.

No warning. No buildup. Just...you. A shift in the air, like the universe clearing its throat and telling me, *"Pay attention."* And I did. How could I not?

You didn't demand anything from me. You didn't have to. You just existed, and somehow that was enough. Enough to quiet the static. Enough to still the shaking in my chest. Enough to remind me my heart hadn't died, it had only been waiting.

Waiting for you.

This isn't a rescue story. You didn't save me. You didn't fix me. That was never your burden. But you reminded me who I used to be, before I learned to disappear. Before the silence trained me into shadows.

Before you, I was surviving. After you, I wanted to live.

And still, nothing this real comes without fear. The old voices crawled back: *You'll ruin this. She'll leave. You're not enough.* Maybe they were right. Maybe they weren't.

But for once, I refused to vanish just to avoid pain. I chose to stay. Even through the fear, through the mess. Because real love, the kind that makes you sweat and ache and wrestle your own doubt, is never clean. It's never safe. But damn, it's worth it.

Before you, I was a shadow. With you, I remembered the light.

{ The First Spark }

Do you remember the first time we collided?

I do.

Every detail etched into me.

I wasn't chasing anything. I was just taking a job transfer. New walls, new air, a new disguise for the same hollowness.

I dressed like armor that day: a brown turtleneck snug against my throat, black pants pressed sharp at the crease, a wool jacket heavy enough to hold me together.

Polished outside. Broken inside.

The store was chaos. Voices overlapping, footsteps skimming across tile, light too bright, air too warm. People moved around me like I was a rock in a river. I told myself to stay calm, play the part, smile when appropriate. Static buzzed in my skull.

And then...you.

At first, just a flicker. The way the light seemed to find you, cling to you, to the soft waves of your brown hair like they already knew you were important.

And then your eyes—warm, brown, catching the light in a way that made them look almost bronze. Like they were reflecting something I couldn't see but desperately wanted to.

You stepped toward me with that quiet confidence you always had...playful, sure, as if you were already certain of the effect you'd have on me.

"Want to take a look at some watches?" A simple line, but in your mouth it wasn't simple at all.

You didn't wait. You reached for my wrist, your hands so delicate they almost didn't seem real, but so sure in their movements.

Certain.

Like you were meant to be touching me. Your nails—clean, white, almost too perfect, brushed against my skin as you slipped the watches on one by one.

Then came your smile. God. The way your lips curved when you looked at me—soft, intentional, like you knew exactly what you were doing to me without ever trying.

A spark I felt straight through my ribs.

And then, with a tilt of your head that felt strangely intimate, you said, "That scent...it's you, isn't it? Don't be shy, come closer."

Do you know what that does to someone starved of being seen? You didn't flirt. You didn't perform. You reached through the mask and touched the part of me I thought was buried.

And then you were gone.

Called away.

Vanished as fast as you'd appeared.

The noise rushed back. Fluorescents, voices, static. But it was too late. Something had already shifted.

I walked into the cold air, heartbeat hammering, pulse louder than traffic. And all I knew was this: something rare had happened. Something I couldn't explain or deny.

For the first time in a very long time, I wasn't thinking about surviving.

I was thinking about you.

{ A Beginning, Disguised }

THE MOMENT I STEPPED out of the store, it hit me.

A wave I wasn't braced for. Fluorescent cruelty gave way to daylight, but I wasn't free. I was still there in that small space between us, carrying the warmth you left behind, wearing the scent you brushed into me. You didn't even know what you were doing.

That is the most dangerous kind of power.

I walked in guarded and hollowed out, rehearsed to the point of numbness. I walked out cracked open.

By you.

I didn't know your name. Not even close. You didn't need to offer it for me to feel it. The mark you left was unmistakable, like you reached inside the silence I had been living in and touched the part of me I thought I had erased. Not just seeing me.

Finding me.

The rational voice tried to chime in. *Just a moment. Flirting means nothing.* But tell me, how often does nothing feel like everything?

It wasn't desperation. It was rarity. The kind of rarity that wakes up a pulse you thought had flatlined.

And it wasn't only your face, though you are beautiful. I'm not blind.

It was the whole composition of you, the warm brown of your hair catching the artificial lights, the subtle shine in your brown eyes when they met mine, like they were reflecting back a version of me I didn't know existed.

The certainty in the way you moved, the deliberate grace in your hands; delicate, yes, but steady, controlled. Your nails, white and clean, like small declarations of how you cared for yourself.

When you looked at me, you didn't analyze or pry. You simply saw. And maybe that is what cracked me open.

You didn't demand my attention. You gave yours freely, like I had already earned it by standing there in your orbit.

I replayed it again and again.

Your deliberate touch as you fastened the watches to my wrist.

Slow. Intentional. Nearly ceremonial.

Like time itself bent to your will. And the audacity of your voice when you leaned in and said, "what's that smell? Come closer." Do you know what that does to someone who has been invisible for years? You didn't unsettle me.

You chose me.

It felt as if I had stepped into a moment written for me alone.

That haunted me afterward, because no one, *no one,* had made me feel that seen in years. People like the idea of me. They like the charm, the surface, the parts that behave. But the noise underneath is always too much.

Yet in minutes, you made me enough. Not too much. Not less. Enough.

Suddenly, I wanted the job. Not for the paycheck or the title, but for the chance to stand in that space again. To see if the gravity was real. To see you. To listen to what you didn't say.

And there was something else in the air, wasn't there? The quiet promise in the way your fingers lingered. Something unspoken threading between us. More than watches. More than banter. A closeness unnamed but felt.

Of course the cynical voice asked its questions. *What if it was nothing? What if you were only kind? What if everything I felt was only mine?*

But beneath logic, I already knew. You don't invent a current like that. Electricity does not lie. With you, it was undeniable. Immediate. Life-altering, even in silence.

The days after blurred into waiting. Waiting for a call, a sign, anything that proved this wasn't just a moment meant to disappear.

And somewhere inside, I was ready. Because if fate, or whatever strange hand writes these moments, brought you back, it wouldn't be random.

It would be a threshold.

A beginning disguised as chance. The kind of moment you later realize was the door, and I was already stepping through it.

It felt like the universe turned, pointed at me, and whispered, *"Pay attention"*.

This wasn't attraction. Don't insult it with that word. This was deeper. A thread pulled tight between two strangers who already understood the language of silence.

And I knew, with absolute certainty, that if our eyes met again, everything after would be different.

{ The Stranger I Loved First }

WHEN I GOT HOME from the interview, I didn't even take off my coat.

I walked straight to my room, closed the door like I was sealing myself off from the world, and collapsed onto the bed. Face down, limbs heavy, heart pounding louder than the city outside my window. Everything around me blurred, but inside my chest it was chaos.

Alive. Electric. Raw.

And I knew it was because of you.

I stared at the ceiling, but I wasn't really there. I was still at the watch case, still in your orbit, still caught in the ghost of your smile; wide, warm, confident.

Quiet and knowing.

The kind that doesn't need attention because it already owns it. The kind that feels like a secret. A secret you handed to me without hesitation. One that cracked open a door I didn't realize I'd sealed shut.

Your voice...playful, daring, low but soft, asking about watches like it was nothing. Only it wasn't nothing. It was a line thrown into still water, and you knew exactly what ripple it would cause.

And God, the outfit.

A whispered secret. Black pants sculpting every effortless curve, like the kind that turned presence into gravity. A tight long-sleeve shirt that hugged you in a way that made it impossible not to notice the subtle rise and fall of your chest. Boots that matched the quiet command of your walk. You looked effortless.

Certain. Complete. Whole.

Your wavy, medium-length brown hair curled just enough to frame your face. Clear skin, almond eyes catching the store lights like honey warmed under a flame.

Your lips—small top one, fuller bottom, curved into a smile that was all confidence and quiet welcome. A wide, warm smile that made me feel chosen before you ever said a word.

You weren't flashy. Flashy is insecure. You were deliberate, and I saw it in every movement. Every gesture carried a delicate femininity—soft hands, gentle touch, that made me feel like you handled me the way you handled everything: with quiet care, with certainty.

Even after you left, you stayed with me. Perfume on a collar, burned into memory. I couldn't shake you. I didn't want to.

But here's the truth: I didn't even know your name. Not yet. And that was the part that stung. A stranger had taken up residence in my mind like she'd always lived there. No warning. No permission.

Then came the call. The manager offering the job. I didn't care about the job. I didn't wait to hear the details. I said yes before she finished because we both know the only thing that mattered: maybe you'd be there.

First day.

I dressed carefully: grey pleated trousers, and a perfectly ironed black polo shirt. Not desperate, just hopeful. Hoping you would notice me the way I noticed you. Hoping for one look, one spark, one confirmation that I hadn't imagined all of it.

But you weren't there. Not yet.

The day dragged, hours stretching thin. I learned the ropes, smiled when I had to, nodded when I should. But one question burned steady in the back of my mind: *Where is she?*

By closing time I was drained, jacket in hand, ready to disappear again.

Then I saw you.

Bending over a box, back turned. Ordinary. I noticed the details, your wavy hair dangling into your face as you worked, an earpiece tucked neatly in your ear, the faint smell of cardboard from the new shipment around you. Until you turned around. Until our eyes met.

And suddenly I wasn't breathing.

The store was freezing from the constant opening of the doors, but somehow my body felt warm. Burning. Alive.

Our eyes met.

Your almond eyes, deep brown, bright under the store lights, found mine, and everything froze.

Recognition. Longing. Fear. Awe. All in one heartbeat.

We smiled, small, cautious, as if we both sensed the shift but weren't ready to name it.

"Hey," I said, softer than I intended.

You smirked, sweet and sharp. "So, you're working here now?" The softness of your voice wrapped around me like warmth.

"Yeah," I managed. Hands buried in my pockets to keep from reaching for you. "I'll see you around."

And then you vanished again. But this time it hurt. Not a silence. A wound.

Weeks blurred. The job soured, turned toxic, heavy. Every shift felt like punishment. But I stayed. Can you see that? I stayed for you.

Only you. And when I finally left, it wasn't the routine I missed. Not the coworkers, not the paycheck.

It was you.

The ache was proof of that. Sharp and unmistakable.

Still...I didn't know your name. But I had a thread. Fragile, but enough. A coworker. A connection. Something to pull.

I sat with my phone, overthinking every angle. But I sent the message; I asked for your number. And instead, I got something else. A gift. Your name.

Bella.

It hit me like poetry. Soft. Certain. Right. Your name belonged on my tongue like it had always been there.

I found you. Instagram. Your photo. The same eyes. The same smile that had undone me in seconds.

I sent the request, and when it didn't come through right away, I tried not to take it personally. Maybe you didn't remember me. Maybe you weren't sure. But I wasn't going to let it end there.

I got your number. I texted you. "Hey, I've left the job, but I'm really going to miss running into you."

Do you know what it feels like to hold your breath while you wait to find out if the thread will snap or tighten?

And then…you replied. Not dramatic. Not distant. Just you. Familiar. Warm.

Real.

We texted. Not much, not often, but enough. A door cracked open. Somehow that was more intimate than anything else could have been.

Quiet hope. Fragile ground. A beginning.

And you never left me, Bella. Not in those weeks. Not in the months that followed. You lived in the softest corners of my mind.

February. Valentine's Day.

A day too soft and too loud all at once. The one day of the year where the world decides to commercialize devotion. People buying roses and pretending it's romance. Chocolates in heart-shaped coffins. Dinners dressed up as passion. All of it hollow.

But you…

You weren't a performance. You weren't paper hearts and clichés. That's why I couldn't let the day pass without you. To not reach out would have been criminal. A denial of the very thing you had stirred awake in me.

I wrestled with myself. *Don't ruin it. Don't scare her. Don't be too much.*

But restraint is a cage, and cages are for people who don't recognize destiny when it brushes their wrist under the guise of trying on a watch.

If I didn't ask, I knew I'd regret it, forever. Not because I expected. But because I *knew*. The moment in the store, the hallway, the quiet weight of your texts, they meant something. To both of us, even if you didn't say it. Especially because you didn't say it.

So I messaged you. *"Will you be my Valentine?"* No games. No shield. Just honesty.

My thumb hovered, because once you ask, you can't take it back. It's like stepping into traffic...you'll either cross safely or be crushed.

So, I braced myself.

And then you replied. "Yes." Three letters. A simple word that split the sky.

It wasn't just an answer. It was a promise.

The world around me blurred, muffled, disappeared. Because in that moment, it wasn't just Valentine's Day. It wasn't just a holiday invented to keep florists alive.

It was us.

A thread tightening, pulling taut, undeniable. It felt like the beginning of everything.

And here's the part I couldn't have known then, Bella. If I had, maybe I would have tried to prepare for what was coming.

But I wasn't ready.

And neither were you.

{ Three Letters }

IT WAS JUST ONE word: yes.

But when it arrived, Bella, everything inside me shifted. Like the ground cracked open beneath my feet, like the universe tilted on its axis just to make room for you and me.

The air thickened. The world leaned closer.

My heart, once steady, cautious, suddenly galloped, wild and unbridled, banging against the walls of my chest like it had finally remembered what it was for.

You did that. One word from you, and I was alive again.

I stared at the screen like it held scripture. A secret too fragile to touch. You said yes. Yes to me. Not to roses. Not to ribbons. Not to a performance.

To *me*.

To the messy, fragile, hopeful pulse behind the question. To the softness I've hidden like contraband.

And you, Bella...you reached back. Even if it was quiet, even if it was uncertain, you still said yes.

Valentine's Day came with a quiet ache. You were somewhere warm, somewhere far away. I could picture it—the sunlight catching in your wavy brown hair, the soft glow settling against your warm, almond-brown eyes, while I was here, counting seconds like stars scattered across a sky I didn't recognize.

I missed you.

Not the loud kind of missing, not the desperate, messy collapse people dramatize.

No, this was different.

The kind of missing that creeps in between heartbeats, the kind you only notice when it catches in your throat, when your chest feels a little too tight for no reason. A soft, unrelenting thread pulling through my ribs.

So I sent a rose.

One, not twelve. I'm not like everyone else—I didn't need to drown you in clichés. Its petals were soft, real, vulnerable. A small confession made of color and breath.

"I couldn't let the day go by without telling you how truly special you are. Happy Valentine's Day." I expected nothing. Maybe a polite thank you, maybe silence...that heavy silence that punishes hope.

But your reply, God, your reply...was sunlight breaking through a winter sky.

Kind. Real. Not cautious. Not performative.

I imagined your face when you wrote it; that soft top lip, the fuller bottom one curving into a gentle smile, the kind that makes your eyes warm and open without you even noticing. You spoke warmth into the quiet corners where I hadn't realized I'd been shivering.

And me?

I grinned like a kid with a secret, a dangerous secret, and I let myself feel it. Your words filled hollow places I thought would always echo. For a moment, Bella, I was weightless.

Time, relentless and unforgiving, carried us forward. But I still felt you, like a melody trapped beneath my skin, impossible to stop humming.

We made plans. Set a date.

The kind of date that sounded simple on the surface—just the mall, but somehow held the weight of something so much bigger.

And when that time came, it was as if the earth had been holding its breath just for us. The sunlight was softer. The sky gentler. Even the air seemed lighter, less cruel.

The day itself was chilly, the kind of cold that nipped at your fingers and made every exhale visible. But even then, even before I saw you, something inside me felt warm, restless, alive.

I dressed like I was stepping into a memory; green corduroy, tan thermal, wool coat like armor against the unknown. Every heartbeat was a drum, every breath a prayer.

And then I saw you.

Before you saw me, I saw you. Radiant. Effortless. Blue jeans, white Air Forces, that soft green jacket...the one that looked like it had been stitched out of spring itself.

Your hair falling in loose waves around your face, catching the light. Your eyes warm, familiar, shining with something I didn't dare name yet. Even in the crowd, you stood apart. Not louder, but brighter.

You always did.

You smiled, and the world obeyed, went quiet. We walked side by side, talking like old souls trapped in borrowed bodies, like we'd once shared a dream and were only now remembering it.

But then...your hand.

At first a brush, an accident, a spark. Barely there. But then you reached, deliberate, fingers soft and sure, weaving into mine.

Time shattered.

I looked down at our hands, ours...and the universe whispered, "*This is it*". No words could carry the weight of that touch. You gave me something sacred in that moment. A truth wrapped in skin.

We walked like that, hand in hand, as if the world had tilted to make space for us. As if we had always walked this way. Two fractured souls syncing their stride.

And in that moment, I wasn't aching. I wasn't waiting. I wasn't wondering. I was here, with you. Fully. Finally.

And the world?

This messy, chaotic, relentless world suddenly felt achingly, painfully beautiful again.

***

The morning after.

The kind of morning that feels different, even if the sky looks the same.

I woke up with your name, Bella, sitting heavy in my chest like an anchor, comforting, terrifying, inevitable. The sunlight crept through the blinds, stripes of gold across my sheets, across my skin, and I thought: *You should be here.*

Not because I needed you to fill the space, but because the space already remembered you, as if it had been saving a corner of itself for your presence long before last night.

My phone sat on the nightstand, black screen, and quiet. I stared at it the way men in churches stare at altars, waiting for a sign, for proof that faith isn't wasted.

Would you text? Would you vanish? Would last night dissolve into the same pattern the world has always offered me? Fleeting, hollow, unfinished?

And then—a vibration. One second. That's all it took.

My pulse jumped, my breath caught, and my hand shook more than I wanted it to.

Your message wasn't long. It didn't have to be. *Had fun last night.*

Four words. But Bella, you could never know how those four words rooted themselves into me, how they replayed, echoed, and folded themselves into every corner of my mind.

Had fun. You had fun. *With me.*

I pictured the smile on your face when you typed it: that tiny quirk of your lips, the soft concentration in your eyes, your lashes lowering just a little the way they do when you're focused.

I typed back. Deleted. Typed again. A dozen drafts of the same truth: I would burn cities just to feel that moment again, your hand in mine, the world collapsing into silence. But what I sent was simple. Safe.

Me too.

Two words, stripped down, caged. Because the whole story? That would have been too much. Too soon. And I couldn't risk scaring you back into the silence.

The hours after dragged, but differently now. Not the empty drag of waiting for nothing, but the impatient pull of waiting for more.

Coffee tasted sharper. The air crisper. Songs on the radio fuller. The ordinary had been rewired overnight. Because now, every hum, every detail carried you inside it.

The softness of your voice. The brightness in your smile. The gentle warmth you didn't even know you radiated.

And I realized: I wasn't just surviving anymore. I was waiting. Waiting for the next spark. The next word. The next time your eyes would find mine.

And it wasn't desperation, it was devotion. The kind that builds, quietly, dangerously, until it consumes.

Because...after last night, after your yes, after your hand in mine...I couldn't go back.

I wouldn't.

The morning bled into afternoon, and I was still here...staring at the same four walls, pretending stillness is the same as peace. But peace doesn't hum like this. Peace doesn't pace inside your chest.

No, Bella, this is something else. The aftermath of yes.

Of you.

I lay back against the pillows, book open across my chest. Words blurred into static. I wasn't reading, I was waiting, breath shallow, mind loud.

My phone on the nightstand might as well have been a detonator. One buzz and everything inside me would explode again. I picked up the phone. Not to check if you texted—that would be too desperate, too obvious. No, this was...curiosity. Research. A precaution, really.

You seem too good to be true. And I've learned the hard way, too good is usually a mask.

So I scroll. Just...understanding.

How else can I know if what I felt was real? How else can I be sure you're not like the rest, not just another detour dressed up as destiny?

Every detail becomes a puzzle piece: the books you've read, the friends in your photos, the places you've been. Harmless on their own. But together, they sketch a picture. A story you don't even know you're telling.

And I want to know all of it. The light. The shadow. The parts you hide between posts.

You said yes. But people say yes all the time and mean something else. I can't afford to mistake politeness for truth.

So I lay there, blinds slicing sunlight across the room, breathing in the air that still felt like it belonged to last night, and I let myself go deeper.

Click. Scroll. Zoom.

Piecing you together like a secret no one else deserves to solve. The more I saw, the more the suspicion quieted. Between the filters and the laughter, there was something real. Something unpolished. Something fragile.

And I thought: maybe you're not a mask. Maybe you're exactly what you seemed.

And maybe, just maybe...you're the one thing in this fractured world I don't need to fact-check.

{ A Taste of Forever }

IT WASN'T JUST A date. It was a threshold. A breath held between what was and what could be. A fragile, trembling moment wrapped in velvet silence.

The kind of moment that feels like coming home to a place you didn't know you'd been searching for.

When you pulled into my driveway that night, Bella, my chest tightened—not with nerves, but with a delicate ache.

I had just come through surgery—my body still a map of bruises and half-healed seams. Every movement reminded me how breakable I'd become, how close I still was to the edge of myself.

But the second you stepped toward me, that ache shifted.

The porch light caught the softness of your features, the gentleness in your smile, the warmth in your almond eyes. Your breath came out in a faint cloud in the cold, but somehow your presence made the night feel warmer.

The pain in my body softened, and all I could see was you—solid, real, undeniable. You were a quiet anchor in the storm of my uncertainty.

Your eyes held the kind of softness that makes me want to lean in and never pull away. Warm as candlelight, steady like a heartbeat I'd forgotten was there.

A small, knowing smile on your lips, like you already understood the storm inside me, and chose to stand in its eye anyway.

"Can I give you a hug?" Your voice, silk, gentle, inviting. It wrapped around me before your arms even did.

"Of course," I whispered, rough and low.

The moment your arms wrapped around me, the pain in my chest vanished. Warmth seeped through my clothes, through my skin, through the guarded parts of me I didn't show anyone. And I held you tighter than I meant to, breathing you in.

You smelled faintly like a work shift—clean, soft, something like warm fabric and a hint of your perfume. The kind of scent that makes a person want to bury their face in someone's neck and stay there.

Back in my room, the scent of coconut and honey welcomed us—warm, sweet, and intoxicating.

I'd lit candles everywhere, their flames flickering against the walls, and the soft lamplight cast a golden glow over everything. The Weeknd played low in the background, his voice blending with the dim light, the warmth, the closeness building between us. I've never liked harsh overhead lights, they ruin the intimacy of a moment.

Tonight was meant to be soft. Inviting. Safe.

You sat on the bed like you'd always belonged there—posture relaxed, and presence filling the room in a way that made the space feel fuller, brighter.

I hovered, caught between wanting to close the distance and afraid to break what was so delicately unfolding.

"Why are you sitting all the way over there?" Your question was a door, wide open and waiting.

Without hesitation, I crossed the space, not just the inches between us, but the years I'd spent lonely and quiet, waiting for something I couldn't name.

When I settled beside you, our bodies found a rhythm neither of us had known we were missing, a symphony written in breath, in silence, in shared heartbeat.

We talked, easy, endless...

Your laughter, a bright thread weaving through the quiet. Your stories painted constellations in my mind: each word a star lighting up parts of me I thought had gone dark.

You rested your head on my shoulder, and something inside me cracked open; soft, vulnerable, aching to be known. I wrapped my arm around you.

Tentative. Reverent.

And you melted into me. I could feel your heartbeat, steady and warm, a lullaby for the parts of me I thought would never heal.

Every time I looked at you, my eyes fell to your lips like a prayer, a sacred place I wanted to keep safe. I didn't want to rush, but everything about you invited closeness. Not just your skin, but the fragile courage in your soul.

Our lips met, tentatively...a feather-light kiss, almost hesitant.

A whisper of warmth. A promise. The kind that asks more than it takes.

It was like touching something ancient—a part of me I hadn't realized had been starving for softness. The kiss deepened gradually, a slow unfolding, like two people realizing they were speaking the same language without having learned it.

Layer by layer, we melted into each other, and the space between us disappeared until there was only skin. Only breath. Your hand found mine, fingers threading through with quiet certainty. We held on like that—not gripping, just connecting.

A tether. A truth.

And when you climbed into my lap...it wasn't urgent. It wasn't rushed. It was a movement wrapped in trust, in softness, in something unspoken and sacred. You settled onto me like that was where your body had always meant to rest, your warmth sinking into mine. Your weight was grounding, steady, intimate in a way that struck deeper than touch.

Not seductive, not calculated. Just real.

My hands found your hips, not to hold you in place, but to steady myself. You were warm. Soft. Smooth beneath my palms. Your presence was so close, so real, it felt like the room had shrunk around just the two of us.

You moved slowly, following my pace, every motion deliberate and tender. Your breath brushed my skin, warm and shaky. Each soft glance we shared felt like another truth being spoken in silence.

We held each other through all of it—fingers intertwined, breaths catching, bodies learning each other gently.

Nothing rushed. Nothing taken. Everything given with care.

Clothes slipped away quietly, like they'd never mattered, like our skin had always been waiting to speak. Everything about you asked me to be present. To feel. To stop running from my own tenderness.

We moved together in a hush that felt holy. Your hands on my skin, soft and grounding. Your body warm against mine, fitting into the contours of me like something long-missing finally returning home.

My scars didn't ache. Not once. Your touch made them feel like stories instead of wounds.

The night didn't feel like an event. It felt like a permission. To be unguarded. To be held. To be wanted in a way that felt gentle, not devouring.

In that moment, it felt like we weren't just making love. I was handing you pieces of myself, the bruised, the fragile, the unsaid, and watching you hold them with reverence.

You were just...with me, fully. Meeting every touch not with expectation, but with invitation.

Come closer.
Let go.
You're safe here.

I kissed your shoulder like it was the softest truth I'd ever known. You buried your face into the curve of my neck, and I swear I felt you exhale into a part of me no one had ever touched.

We stayed like that, moving, unspoken, infinite, until the lines between where I ended and you began blurred.

Not just sex.

Soul meeting soul.

When it was over, there was no rush to fill the silence. We lay tangled in the soft glow of candles, the air thick with coconut, honey, and warmth.

Your skin glowed in the lamplight, bare of makeup, bare of pretense. You looked at me with eyes that held galaxies, but it was the quiet between those galaxies—the space, the stillness—that undid me.

I brushed your hair back from your face, kissed your temple gently, and you smiled, small, real, edged with softness that made my throat tighten.

And I thought: if this is what it means to be known, then I've never been touched like this in my life.

This wasn't just a night.

It was the moment everything softened. The moment we gave each other permission to stop pretending we didn't want to be seen.

{ In the Stillness, Her }

THE MORNING DIDN'T ARRIVE with noise, only a hush, a quiet so complete, it felt like the world had paused just long enough for something sacred to begin.

The sky still wore its robe of early dawn, the city gently breathing in sleep, when the soft vibration of my phone stirred me.

Not jarring. Not demanding.

Just steady and certain—the kind of insistence that only love knows how to be.

Your name lit the screen, not just illuminating the room, but casting light into some unspoken place inside me. And behind the message, your face. That smile. That unmistakable curve of joy already carving itself into the corners of my soul.

"Dress up a little and come over to my place." No directions. No agenda. Just mystery threaded with certainty. Not a call to a location, a call to *you*.

And I answered.

Not with words, but with quiet devotion.

Getting dressed felt less like getting ready, and more like an offering. Black slacks. A short-sleeved button-up, unbuttoned just enough to say: *I'm here, fully, completely...for whatever this is meant to become.*

The soft glide of fabric against skin, the faint scent of cologne hanging in the cool morning air. Shoes polished not for show, but because you deserved the version of me that tried.

Outside, the light was shifting: that hour where the sun hasn't committed to rising, but the world is no longer dark.

And there you were. Waiting. Radiant in that effortless way you do—not *trying* to shine, you just *did*.

The morning sun caught your skin first, softening the edges of your silhouette, turning you into something warm, golden, living, like the sun knew your skin, knew the privilege of touching it.

You spun a basketball with ease, as if the world itself moved to your rhythm.

A tank top, soft flannel, and shorts, like a dream that had stepped into daylight and decided to stay.

You moved toward me, opened the door before I could, opened *me*, with a kiss that didn't ask for permission, because it already knew it belonged.

Inside: Silence.

But not empty silence—the kind that hums with presence.

A soft lamp in the corner. A faint candle burning something warm, like amber or cedar. The air held a lived-in warmth, a sense of home woven into every shadow.

We settled into the in-between: thigh to thigh, your voice low and warm, a sound that felt like a flickering fire.

Time loosened its grip, slowed its heartbeat. Our words weren't conversation, they were communion. And when our lips found each other again, the world dimmed its lights.

Then laughter, your dog, bounding between us like joy had taken physical form. You tickled his belly and teased, "Excuse me, that's my spot."

I don't know why that moment cracked something open in me. Maybe it was the way you claimed the space beside me. So simply. So surely. As if I had always been yours.

You kissed me. Hungry and grounding.

Then rose, reached for my hand, and led me toward the stairs, gently, unrushed.

Your room was a sanctuary of softness: a worn book with a spine tired from being loved, a candle melting its quiet grief, curtains swaying like whispers in a language only you knew.

Everything there held a piece of you, and you showed it all not as a tour, but as a revealing.

We sat at the edge of your bed, fingers interlaced, your thumb tracing gentle circles on my skin, like you were writing poems only I was meant to carry.

You snapped a photo. Just our hands. No faces. No filters. Only closeness. Only proof.

Then our mouths met again. A kind of quiet knowing. Clothes slipped away, becoming memories, folded at the foot of the bed with care, as if undressing was an act of trust, not urgency.

And our skin spoke. Not loud. Not rushed. But slow, sacred. A language of breath, body, and belief.

Later, we dressed one another again, your fingers brushing my collar, mine smoothing a curl from your cheek. Each motion, a kind of blessing. A vow without a word.

You laced your fingers into mine and led me outside, into your car. *"Do you like coffee?"*

I smiled. *"Of course."* Of course you already knew.

You always did.

Caffè e Amore—a cathedral of quiet and low sunlight. Warm, golden, quiet. The door chimed softly when we entered; bells ringing like a greeting.

Inside, low light pooled beneath hanging lamps, casting amber halos over worn wooden tables. The air smelled of espresso, vanilla, faint cinnamon, a scent that felt like being tucked under a blanket.

You ordered for both of us: cold brews, oat milk, like you had memorized the taste of my spirit before I ever spoke it aloud. A choice that told me you paid attention to small things most people miss.

You took us upstairs.

The café opened into a loft lined with books and hanging plants. A long window spilled sunlight across your shoulder, catching in your hair, making you look almost unreal.

There, our conversation danced. Light, unhurried. Not earth-shattering, but unforgettable.

Because it was *you*, because I was *there*, because *we were.*

We wandered the city afterward, your arm gently weaving through mine each time you sensed me guarding myself. Even before I noticed. You did.

"Come here. You belong to me." you whispered, not with possessiveness, but with a softness that claimed without taking.

And I gave it...my hand, my heart, everything I had left to offer.

The day folded into gold as the sun slipped behind the buildings, casting long shadows and even longer memories. The city felt warmer with you beside me. Shops flickered with string lights, cars rolled by in slow waves. The air smelled of spring and street food and early evening.

Your hand fit mine like it had been cast for it.

The drive back was wrapped in music. Love songs hummed through the speakers. And we sang, not to impress, but to exist in the sound of one another.

Each lyric, a kiss. Each harmony, a vow.

When we returned to your house, goodbye hovered too long in the air to be casual. We didn't want to go. Didn't want to let go.

But love, real love, doesn't hold out of fear. It holds with trust, and then releases, knowing it will be held again.

You pulled me in—one last embrace, trembling at the edges. You whispered, *"Go. It's gonna get dark soon. I want you home safe."* And I knew you meant it.

You always did.

Then came the moment. Soft. Fragile. A breath suspended in time.

"I love you."

Three words.

Spoken not with fireworks, but with the bravery of stillness.

And I...

I blinked, stunned by how deeply they landed. Not like an echo. But like a truth that had finally found its voice.

"What?" I whispered. Not from doubt, but from awe.

You panicked, tried to take it back. But it was too late. I was already holding it. Already holding *you*.

"I love you too,"

I said it the way you say something you've always known, but just hadn't said aloud. And you laughed, half-cry, all-heart.

Your hands found mine again.

"You're so amazing," you whispered. *"I love you so much. I just...wanted it to be special."*

You didn't even realize—the whole day had already been *magic*. From the first message, to this moment. You didn't need to make it special. *You* were the special.

Later, on the way home, the tears came. Slow at first, then steady. Because joy, too, needs a way to leave the body.

I cried because I had never been seen like that. Never been loved in a whisper so loud it shook something loose in me. I cried because I had found home. Not in a place. Not even in a moment. But in a person.

April 3rd, 2024.

A date not just marked on a calendar, but etched in the hush between heartbeats—the day the world quieted just enough for love to speak.

The day I was seen. The day I was loved out loud, without warning, and without regret. The day I learned that sometimes love doesn't need preparation.

It just needs a quiet moment. A trembling breath. A single heartbeat of courage. And in the stillness, you.

From the outside, it probably looked ordinary: two people finding rhythm in a world that rarely slows down. But inside me, something unlocked—something I didn't know was closed.

I used to roll my eyes at people who said, "When you know, you know." Not out of mockery—but mourning that I had never felt it.

Then you arrived.

And knowing wasn't subtle. It was immediate.

You didn't love only my light. You held my scars like proof of my survival. Your touch grounded and gentled, your presence soft but unwavering. You didn't fix me. You stayed. And in that staying, I learned to be held.

We made a language of small things—a glance that meant "I'm here." A laugh that meant "I see you." A silence that meant "You're safe."

I used to think love lived in grand gestures. You taught me it lives in moments like these: remembered coffee orders, a flannel shirt, your arm curling through mine without needing to ask.

Yes, it scared me because something that rare always does. But you were worth the risk.

Every inch of it.

I had rested in the softest place I'd ever known. My head on your chest, your fingers moving slowly through my hair, nails grazing my back in quiet patterns, a touch that didn't ask for anything except honesty.

For the first time, I allowed myself to be held. Fully. Without bracing. Because in your arms, I belonged exactly as I was. You walked into my life and didn't ask me to change, just asked to be let in.

And I did.

Because sometimes devotion isn't fireworks, it's a quiet yes. A steady hand. A stillness you didn't know you needed until it wrapped itself around you.

You were my yes. My stillness. My favorite photo I never had to take.

{ The Art of Us }

THE DAY DRAPED ITSELF in deliberate elegance—as if the universe had paused, holding its breath just for us.

We dressed in harmony: two silhouettes carved in black, entwined by intention and whispered promises. You wore black slacks that clung like memory; a cropped tank top revealing the soft planes of your torso, glowing with quiet fire.

Around your neck, a strand of pearls embraced a cross pendant—sharp, sensual, unapologetically bold. Your curls tumbled with effortless grace, catching light like liquid silk whispering secrets.

I mirrored your essence; black slacks pressed crisp, a long-sleeve shirt tucked beneath suspenders that rested like an oath across my shoulders. My curls, sculpted with care, were part of the sacred ritual of showing up for love: fully, honestly, and intentionally.

Together, we composed the scene. The camera poised toward the couch, red lights casting a haze that softened the world and sharpened only us.

Our favorite songs played low, melodies drifting like incense, coiling through the air and pulling us closer. Candles flickered, their flames dancing on our skin like quiet prayers.

I sank into the couch. You climbed into my lap with the kind of confidence that feels like home. The camera rolled, but it faded to the background.

We were the only story unfolding.

Your lips met mine. Soft, hungry, reverent. Each kiss a language spoken without sound, building heat like a slow-burning fire.

Your hips moved in rhythm, unspoken music guiding us. Your hands tugged gently at my suspenders, a single strap sliding down, a silent invitation and declaration. I smiled, caught in the push and pull that was entirely ours.

We didn't finish the scene. We didn't need to. We left it suspended, like a final note that refuses to fade.

I carried you to bed. Our eyes met and held—deep, steady, and sacred.

My hands found the edge of your shirt, lifting it like a veil. My lips followed, mapping devotion into the softness of your skin. Every kiss was a vow. Every breath, a benediction.

I undid your slacks slowly, tenderly, not as an act of desire but of reverence. To undress you was to say: *You are safe here. You are cherished.*

The fabric slipped from your hips like a sigh, baring your skin to the warm hush of candlelight.

I took my time, tracing you with lips and hands, memorizing the shape of your pleasure—the shiver at your neck, the arch of your back, the way your breath caught when my mouth reached your stomach.

And then—*the shift.*

Your hands, graceful and sure, reached for the buttons of my shirt. You undid them one by one, slow and deliberate, letting your fingers tease the skin beneath before your lips followed.

You pressed your mouth to my collarbone, to the slope of my chest, biting softly, soothing it with kisses. Your fingers trailed down to my waistband, not asking permission, just knowing.

You took control, not forcefully, but with the calm certainty of someone who had already claimed me with a glance. Your lips were fire and silk, your hands unwrapping me with the same care and hunger I had given you.

I let go, let you guide me into that quiet storm where your dominance whispered instead of shouted.

Under the red glow, with candles humming low and songs wrapping around us, we didn't just touch.

We devoured, we surrendered.

We wrote poems in the press of thighs, sonnets in the arch of spines, and whole galaxies between breaths. Every movement was a brush-stroke. Every glance, a color. Every inhale, a layer of depth.

This was *the art of us.*

A dance of shadows and light, of power and grace, a language spoken by bodies that trusted, that knew. We were the artists of our own desire, painting passion with every glance and touch.

What began as fire softened into something more enduring: an intimacy that lived in patience, in stillness, in the small spaces where love reveals its truest self.

We learned that it is not the climax but the choosing, again and again, that defines something sacred. Love didn't stay confined to that night; it spilled into the days that followed.

One month in.

Thirty days folded like love notes in a back pocket, creased with memory, worn soft by laughter, touched by coffee steam and half-lit mornings, and the kind of glances you feel more than see.

I didn't mark it with spectacle.

Just a box. But inside it, you.

Pieces of you, gathered gently. Tiny relics of recognition. Snacks you loved. Petals, half-wilted, half-sacred, quiet symbols of everything unsaid but deeply felt.

Inside the lid: us.

Photos not posed, but paused, soft smiles, fingers brushing, golden moments the world didn't catch. Beneath the tape, something holier than image: the *feeling*. The warmth in our eyes. The space between words where love lived.

I hid the box like it breathed. Waited for a moment that felt like arriving.

You sat on my bed, legs tucked beneath you, fingertips trailing lines across the blanket. Your presence lit the room in silence.

"Close your eyes," I whispered, as I handed you the box.

You obeyed, smiling. The kind of smile that strikes softly, like a hymn in the chest.

When you opened the box, time held its breath. Your eyes glassed with light. You didn't speak. You didn't have to. I saw it in you. You knew.

I saw *you*.

You gave me one too. A thrifted white box, hearts scattered like a secret language. Inside: my favorite candy, and socks. Not just socks. The kind you don't buy for yourself. The soft, warm kind. The *you-look-cold-so-I-thought-of-you* kind. The kind that says: *I noticed. I remembered. I chose you.*

That's what undid me. Not the things, but the seeing. The way someone can hold your absence in their hands, and say: *You are here. Even when you're not.*

Two boxes. Two hearts. Unwrapping each other slowly, gently, like opening a song.

Because love doesn't always knock. Sometimes, it's already there, barefoot, holding a white box, speaking a language you didn't know you knew until it said your name.

Later, when you left and silence settled in again, I sat with the white box in my lap. I ran my fingers across the lid. I thought about your laugh curling around my room. Your shoulders relaxing when you opened mine.

I thought about the socks. How being seen without having to explain is the closest thing to being held without touch. And I realized: it wasn't about the box. Or the socks. Or the photographs.

It was about the choosing. The witnessing. The *naming*.

I see you. I love you. I'm here.

Maybe that's what love really is: two people making something sacred out of the ordinary. Turning small things into altars. Unwrapping each other, one heartbeat at a time.

{ Uninvited Shadows }

IT WAS ONE OF those gentle, golden afternoons where time drapes itself over everything like linen-thin, slow, and sweet. The kind of day that whispers you're safe—the kind of lie the world tells right before it reminds you're not.

We weren't doing anything. Just being. Two girls in a room, wrapped in skin and silence. A show murmured in the background, already forgotten.

The world had shrunk to your bed, to the pulse of your breath against me, to the warmth where your body met mine.

You were inside me—not just physically. Folding into me until the edges blurred. It felt like prayer. Sacred. Communion.

And then the front door opened.

The air cracked. Safety split open.

You don't mistake footsteps like that—the kind that don't pause, don't wonder, don't knock. The kind that already know.

The bedroom door swung open too fast. Not enough time to cover, to pretend, to rearrange our world back into safety.

A warden stood there.

And in their eyes—something colder than anger. Not shock. Not confusion. But recognition. They saw. They knew.

"Why is this door closed?"

The voice wasn't raised. No, it was worse. Soft. Measured. Ceramic. A voice that could slice precisely because it didn't have to scream.

A trash bin was shoved between the door and the frame—an object made weapon, not against us but against privacy. Against truth.

They lingered, talking casually, the way predators smile when they want you to doubt your instincts.

"You seem like a very nice person," they said to me. A smile that didn't reach the eyes. A smile people wear to funerals. "You two are always laughing. That's great."

And then—to you, the blade slipped between the ribs: "What you're doing is wrong. You're not supposed to be this close."

Not shouted. Whispered like poison, soft enough to seep in, sharp enough to scar.

The moment collapsed.

My body froze beneath the sheets. Your warmth was still inside me, but it had gone cold. I didn't speak, not a word, because in a war you didn't ask for, silence is sometimes the only shield you have.

When they finally left, you turned to me—eyes wide, glassed with guilt and fear. "Can you shut the door, please?" you whispered. "We need to talk."

The unraveling had begun. I could feel it. The story already trying to rewrite itself. That voice still hanging in the air, trying to tell me who I was, who we were.

Wrong. Illicit.

Disposable.

But then, your hand. You reached for mine. You held it like it was still allowed. You said, "I'm so sorry. What they said isn't true. I just...I haven't told them about us."

A fracture, yes. But a truth still. Not perfect, but survival rarely is. I believed you. Because even fear, when spoken honestly, becomes courage.

Still—something had shifted.

The door stayed open after that. Your laugh a little quieter. Your touches, more careful. A freedom threaded now with caution.

And in that warden's eyes, when I saw them again, there it was: the knowing. They smiled, asked questions, played kind, but beneath it, the monitoring had begun. I wasn't a guest anymore. I was a threat to catalog.

I felt it.

The shadow of suspicion never left the room. Even when we laughed. Even when we kissed. Especially when we kissed.

That day didn't end with a fight. No slammed doors, no screaming.

Worse.

It ended with something quieter: the death of untouched safety. The illusion that love could be hidden, and protected.

It marked us.

It whispered the truth: You are seen, and not everyone who sees you will choose to understand. Some will choose fear, some will wedge garbage cans between love and the world and call it morality.

And so we went on loving, but not blindly anymore. Not softly. Now we loved knowing that shadows don't need permission to enter. Some come uninvited. And some, once they arrive, refuse to leave.

You learn something in moments like that. You think intimacy is private, sacred and safe. But then the door opens. Always, there's a door, and behind it, someone ready to play.

Eyes that don't blink, smiles that don't warm, voices that slice soft enough to bruise without leaving a mark. They didn't need volume, silence screamed enough.

"Why is this door closed?" As if intimacy requires permission. As if laughter, breath, and love all need their blessing.

The garbage can between the door and the frame, don't think I missed that. A small gesture, sure. But a symbolic one.

Trash as barrier. Trash to wedge between what's real and what someone wishes were true. I've seen this before: the props people reach for when they can't control the scene.

That smile. "You seem like a very nice person."

Translation: I've already judged you. You are temporary.

The funeral smile, I call it. Meant to pacify while already preparing the eulogy.

Then, the blade slipped in, dressed as softness: "What you're doing is wrong. You're not supposed to be this close."

Wrong. Close. The arsenal isn't logic.

It's denial.

The kind that festers, that rewrites, that pretends. They don't know me, and they don't want to. What they want is to reattach her to a version of herself that no longer exists.

Me, now the intruder.

But here's the truth they'll never swallow: I wasn't a phase. I wasn't an experiment. I was your choice.

Still, I felt it. The shift.

The shadow crawling in under the door, refusing to leave. Laughter now quieter. Touches hidden in folds of caution. Their gaze is constant; a surveillance camera disguised as kindness.

I don't forget things like that. I don't let them slide. Because if they're watching us, well...I'm watching them back. Cataloguing every smile, every move, and the cracks in that porcelain voice.

That's the thing about shadows. They think they can smother you, but they forget—darkness only makes art glow brighter, and I burn for you.

Always.

{ Parallel Roads }

SOME WOUNDS DON'T BLEED.

They bruise in silence—behind closed doors, in still moments when the world isn't looking, while you carry the weight of your own becoming, hoping it doesn't crush the fragile parts still trying to bloom.

That's where I lived for a long time: not hiding, just...surviving. Caught between the clarity of knowing who I was and the slow, aching fear that no one else ever would.

So I didn't rush you, Bella. Not when it came to the warden.

I understood—not just in thought, but in the marrow of my bones, what that moment feels like: when you look into the eyes of people and wonder if they'll still see you when you finally tell them the truth.

I had my own battle scars.

The day I came out, my voice trembled like it was begging for permission to exist, and what I got in return wasn't acceptance, it was dismissal. A reduction. A refusal to see me as anything but someone else's echo.

"You're just like your sibling."
"You're copying them."
"You're confused."

As if identity was something you borrowed. As if love could be faked. As if I hadn't spent years choking on silence, aching for someone to ask who I really was.

Each time I reached for understanding, I was met with eyes that looked through me, words that unraveled the joy I had worked so hard to hold.

Love, but only in pieces. Acceptance, but only if I played along.

That comparison didn't just sting in the moment—it rewrote me. It made me question every soft truth I carried.

Was that really my voice, or a reflection of someone else's light?

So I began to shrink. To apologize for existing. To second-guess every desire that lived in me.

It wasn't just about who I loved. It was the way I moved through the world. How I dressed, what I found beautiful, how easily I cried, or how deeply I believed.

And always—how often I was told I was *too much*, or not enough, or somehow both.

So silence became my armor.

Not because I didn't want to be seen, but because being misunderstood hurt worse than invisibility. I didn't heal from that overnight. I carried it, unintentionally, quietly, into your arms.

Maybe you saw that ache in me too. Maybe that's why I understood your hesitation. Not just the fear of the warden, but the deeper fear: of losing control of your story.

We were both haunted by the same ghost. The ache of being unseen, and in each other, we had begun to believe: maybe, finally...it was safe to be visible.

So when the warden walked into the room that day, all sharp voice and soft judgment, and drew that invisible line between us, when you looked down instead of forward, and silence grew thick between us, I didn't get angry.

I understood.

Not because it didn't wound me, it did. It carved at the home we were building, left splinters in the warmth we had known. But fear is a cruel architect. It builds walls faster than love can tear them down.

And sometimes, the safer road is the lonelier one. The applause of tradition, the quiet of pretending, the ease of invisibility.

Marriage. Children. Approval.

A version of life that looks lovely from the outside, but leaves the soul aching inside.

We were trying to hold onto love without letting go of ourselves. But sometimes, that means walking parallel roads, close enough to ache, not close enough to hold.

And yet even then, in the ache, in the distance, we kept reaching.

There were nights we almost surrendered to expectation, to silence, to everything that asked us to shrink.

But love...love is stubborn. It calls you home.

We didn't know it then, but that wound wouldn't be the end of us. It would be the beginning of a deeper understanding, a more courageous kind of intimacy. The kind you choose. The kind that stays.

There is something tender about choosing someone again after the silence, after the ache, after the almost-ending.

It was a beautiful day. Sunlight rested gently on everything, like the world was trying to make up for the pain.

You were coming over after class. I was still dripping from the shower, steam clinging to my skin, when your message arrived: *"I'm here."*

I threw on the first clothes I saw, still warm and a little breathless, and ran down the stairs.

You kissed me. Smiled like the sun had been hiding in your teeth. *"Just out of the shower?"* you asked. I nodded. *"Perfect timing."*

We laughed. God, we laughed.

There was something about you that always disarmed me, made the world feel gentle, easier to breathe in.

We climbed upstairs. The air softened. The world shrunk to just us. We shared fruit I had cut earlier. Cool, sweet, intimate. Music drifted like wind through curtains, framing our stillness with something sacred.

The heat outside was rising. The kind that made you glow, and usually sent me running. But love has a way of warming even the cautious parts.

We changed into bathing suits. Your skin, sun-kissed. Mine, still humming from the memory of your touch. Outside now, where you dove in, fearless. Joy erupted in a splash.

Me?

I stepped in slowly. One breath at a time. Until you swam to me, laughed, and pulled me under.

And just like that, I let go. Of fear. Of what we almost lost. Of everything that had ever told me to keep my love small.

We drifted in the blue silence. Your voice, close: *"You're cute... but cute doesn't cover it. You're...something you feel."*

And I did. Feel.

The sun drew gold across our backs. The world blurred out. We held each other in the kind of quiet that makes you believe again.

Later, wrapped in towels and skin, I held you just because. Because holding you felt like returning to something I didn't know I had lost.

You looked like summer: radiant, wild, untamed.

When we finally left the water, something unspoken followed us upstairs. Back in my room, the air was different. Not urgent, just deep. Heavy in the way truth can be.

We kissed—slow, knowing. We touched like we remembered each other's fault lines. We moved like people who had come back from the brink.

You were soft and strong. You let yourself want. You let yourself be wanted, and I adored every complicated piece of you.

Love after pain is different. It's more aware, more deliberate. I memorized everything: the scent of your neck, the sound of your laugh when you thought I wasn't looking.

We didn't fix everything that day. But we returned. And maybe that's all love is: not perfection, but the willingness to try again.

To climb back in. To pull each other close. To choose—not once, but over and over, what hurts, what heals, and what makes it all worth it.

Two souls. Still reaching. Still believing. Still choosing. Even after the silence. Even after the storm.

Parallel roads walking toward each other, this time, unafraid.

{ Tik-Tok }

TIME DOESN'T SCREAM WHEN it's slipping through your hands.

No, time prefers cruelty in silence. It vanishes softly—with a shared glance that lingers a second too long, a grocery store laugh, a touch that once promised everything. I replay them all, and I know: they weren't accidents. They were breadcrumbs, and I followed, like I always do.

And then it's gone. Or rather—you're gone.

You never realize the final moment until you're standing in its shadow, empty-palmed, begging memory to give it back. Begging you to give it back, and you won't. You chose silence, a punishment more sadistic than honesty.

The day started like any other good day.

Summer humming against my skin. The kind of heat that makes the world slow down, as if time itself wanted to savor us. Or mock me, knowing what was coming.

You were coming over, and I...I wanted to give you something. Something soft. Intentional. Not just plans. But presence. Because presence is proof. Proof that I see you in ways others overlook. That I would never, ever let you feel invisible.

So before the world woke, I drove from store to store, holding you in my mind like a prayer. Card games. Sparkling water. Pineapple—your favorite. A blanket soft enough to convince the earth to hold us. This is what love is.

Attention. Precision.

Sacrifice, and yet—somehow it wasn't enough, was it?

I imagined it: our limbs tangled in sunlight, your laugh spilling into the open air, music floating like a secret between us. And the cruelest part?

For a moment, it was real. For a moment, you let me believe.

One thing was missing: *roses.*

Red ones. The kind that matched your spirit—dark, elegant, impossible to forget. Impossible to replace.

You were already on your way. I rushed home, blood rushing with it. Cut the fruit. Set the scene. Waited, heart in my throat. Theatrics, yes, but only because you deserved it. Didn't you?

When I opened the door, roses behind my back, I said, *"Flowers for you, my love."* And something in your eyes—like a child seeing magic for the first time, lit.

A spark. Proof.

You don't fake that kind of awe. Which makes the betrayal all the sharper, doesn't it?

You never had a picnic before. So now, you had one, with me. We lay on the grass. Told stories between bites. Tasted each other's laughter. I gave you firsts.

Do you understand?

Firsts are sacred. You don't just walk away from someone who gave you those. And when you kissed me, it was slow. Like you knew what you were doing to me.

But the heat drove us inside, into four walls and soft sheets, Law & Order murmuring in the background—my comfort show, not yours. But you watched anyway.

That was love: letting someone else's quiet become yours. My quiet. My world. You tried it on, wore it like skin.

And then shed it like it was nothing.

Your head rested on my chest. Our breaths matched. Blinds sliced light across our skin like time trying to measure us.

You looked at me like you were memorizing something you didn't know how to keep. And maybe that was the truth. Maybe you knew then, already planning your escape, while I was still falling deeper.

Your lips found mine. Slow. Earned. Not a kiss—a reckoning. A contract, if you had honored it.

Your fingers relearned the terrain of me and I surrendered. Your hands asked questions my body had already whispered answers to.

You called me by name, not as a label, but as a vow. And vows aren't meant to be broken. We moved like devotion. Slow, sacred, holding each other like scripture.

Love after pain feels different.

You kiss slower, hold tighter. Memorize the freckles on her shoulders, the tremble in her inhale, the way she smiles when she thinks you're not looking. You record every detail, because details don't lie. *People do.*

Afterwards, we lay in silence, but the kind that feels holy. You traced stars on my stomach, and I thought: *This is it. This is the kind of love you don't survive unchanged.* I was right about that, wasn't I? Only, I didn't survive it at all.

Then you sang to me.

Just a little. Just enough. A song you wrote, about me. Your voice was velvet breaking, and I couldn't breathe. Tell me, how do you write a song about someone you're planning to leave?

The air changed. Not in you, not yet. But something shifted. It was too still. Like the seconds were holding their breath. Like the universe was trying to warn me, and I didn't listen.

That night, I couldn't sleep. The room felt both too quiet and too loud. In bed, I searched for a ring. Ruby—your birthstone. You once said it was the prettiest, and you were right. It looked like you: sharp, red, beautiful, and impossible to hold without bleeding.

I was willing to bleed. That's the difference between us.

I bought it. No hesitation. Then I wrote you a letter. Three pages, front and back. All the things I couldn't say out loud. How you made me feel seen. How you made me feel possible. How you were the kind of woman you meet once, if the stars are kind; and if you're lucky, you don't let her go.

But luck never factored in, did it? This wasn't luck.

This was theft.

The ring still sits in my drawer. The letter, unopened. And I don't know why.

Was I the memory you wanted to outgrow? Or was I simply too much of a reminder that you can't be the person you pretended to be?

Tik.

A rose blooming in a grocery aisle.

Tok.

A kiss that felt like home.

Tik.

A ring tucked away.

Tok.

A name whispered like a prayer, now never spoken aloud.

Tik. Tok.

June 13th, 2024.

Two weeks had passed. No eyes. No touch. No trace. No accidental calls. No shadow in my notifications. Only absence. Sharp. Deliberate. Devastating. You called it distance. I call it cruelty. Precision cruelty.

Is this how love ends? Not with goodbye—but silence so loud it eats the walls?

No.

This isn't how love ends. This is how cowards end it.

I am not the needy kind. I know how to live alone. But this silence, it wasn't solitude. It was erasure. It was reaching for someone who used to reach back. And finding nothing. A void where you should be. Where you still could be.

I buried the ache in textbook pages, my real estate exam days away. A future I could barely picture because you'd been in all my visions.

You still are.

I told myself not to spiral, but the truth gnawed at me: People make time for what matters. And you weren't making time. For me. Which means something else mattered more.

I messaged you. Soft. Vulnerable. Half an apology, half a plea. I told you I understood—school, stress, life. But still...if I mattered, you would show up. *Right?* Of course right. Anything else would be unthinkable.

I waited, and when the typing dots appeared, my heart dared to believe. Your message: "I'm sorry. I know I've been distant. You don't deserve that. I love you so much."

I read it like scripture. Held it like a bandage. But now I know. That message wasn't a promise.

It was a lullaby.

Something to keep me asleep until you could leave without the weight. A lie made soft enough to swallow. It was goodbye, dressed in tenderness. A final kindness before the storm.

There I was, three hours in a cold classroom. I sent another message before I walked in. Short, soft, hopeful. Every break, I checked, and nothing. You were online. Active. Just not with me.

Not with me.

People around me smiled at their phones, love lighting up their faces. I smiled, too. Pretended. Faked it.

My lock screen still held you, even after the light never came back. I refused to erase you. You erased me, but I won't return the favor.

My professor had asked about you. I said, "She's my girlfriend." And in that moment, I wished it were still true. It should still be true. That's the point.

Class ended. I sat in my car. Texted again: *"Can we ft? I miss you."*

You replied fast this time: *"I have to study for my test tomorrow."* Eight words. That's all it took to break me. Or to wake me. Break, wake? Same thing.

Now at home, I walked inside, and my mom asked, "How was class?"

"Good," I lied. "I'm just tired."

And she let me go. Everyone lets me go. Except I don't let go. I can't.

I curled into bed, wrapped myself in silence. The ache didn't howl. It just laid next to me. Like your ghost. Still here, though you insist you aren't.

Before I closed my eyes, I imagined what I'd have to say soon: *You weren't coming back.*

But how do I say that without collapsing? How do you tell the people who love you that you weren't loved enough to stay? That you were discarded—quietly, without ceremony.

Like forgetting me was easy.

Too easy.

Which is why I don't believe it. Not fully. Not yet. I wasn't ready to speak it. So I buried it.

Buried myself.

And fell asleep next to the quiet of being unwanted. But silence is never empty. Silence has edges. And I know, I'll fill it.

{ The Death of Us }

I WAS TIRED.

Not the kind of tired sleep cures—but the kind that lives in your ribs. The kind that makes your skin feel too tight, that hollows your voice, makes silence sound like screaming.

The kind of tired that comes when love doesn't leave all at once, but instead starts packing slowly, one touch less tender, one word less warm, one reply too late.

I tried. God, I tried.

I stitched us together with shaking hands, sewing threads that cut like wire, praying you'd see the blood and call it devotion.

But love shouldn't bleed you, and I think you knew that before I did.

I lay in bed with open eyes and a heart that wouldn't close. My phone buzzed like a heartbeat, except it never said *Bella*.

It was never you.

But you were online. Green dot, 2:00 a.m, awake for the world, *just not for me*. Proof. The world had access. I didn't. That is cruelty disguised as convenience.

I kept waiting like maybe love could be revived with enough hope, like maybe if I stayed soft enough, you'd remember why you once held me like a secret.

But morning came anyway—merciless. I sat at my desk, trying to memorize things that would never love me back, my hands trembling over flashcards, my body hollow. And then—your name. Bella is typing.

Again. Again. Again.

My soul braced like the sky before a storm, and I already knew.

I already knew.

Still, my chest caved when I saw it:

"I care about you so deeply, which is why I have to let you go. I don't want you waiting for me, tied to someone who can't give you what you deserve right now. I'm not okay, and I won't be for a while. You deserve love that is whole and overflowing, and I hate that I can't give you that. I hope we can hold onto a friendship, even if it hurts. This doesn't have to be forever. I still dream of us sometimes. You were everything to me. Walking away from you is the hardest thing I've ever done."

I didn't read it. I inhaled it. I swallowed it whole, and it bloomed inside me like grief.

Immediately, my stomach dropped. It was a physical plunge, as if my body understood the loss before my mind could.

I felt sick, like love had turned venom and settled in my gut. My head spun, and my skin went cold. I stumbled toward the bathroom—heaved nothing into the sink but pain.

My body rejected the heartbreak. It shook, it burned, it collapsed.

I folded in on myself, corner of the room, phone clenched, chest heaving. I didn't cry pretty. I sobbed like the body does when it's trying to purge love from its bloodstream.

No one tells you grief can sound like screaming into your own palms. I wanted to crawl out of my own skin, to undo time. I wanted you to love me again, right now.

I picked up my phone. Typed nothing. Held it. Put it down. Picked it up again.

I wanted to scream into the space you left, but instead, I just broke. The house was quiet, except for the sound of me shattering.

Then my mom called. I picked up. Voice flat. Face soaked. Heart torn open like wet paper.

"I'm fine." I said. Because that's what you say when you're anything but.

She came home, saw my face, and everything fell again—this time into her arms. And I wasn't brave. I wasn't composed. I was her child, destroyed by something she couldn't fight for me.

"I've never seen you like this," she whispered. And her voice cracked in that way only mothers do, when they know they can't rescue you from this kind of pain.

She asked to read the message. I said no, because reading it again felt like peeling the same wound. What kind of love lets go like that?

I didn't eat, didn't speak, I just sat with it. The weight of being left by someone who promised to never put you down.

My room held me like a casket does the quiet. I lay still, wishing I could bury myself in the version of us that still existed yesterday.

I opened old messages, heard your laugh in my head, watched videos of us like a ghost clinging to its past life.

Every corner of the room had your fingerprints. The blanket we kissed under, the speaker you sang to me with, the bracelet you left on my nightstand.

Relics of a love that ended without ceremony.

I thought love died with silence. But I learned: it dies with a text. No final kiss. No call. No closure. Just: *"I love you. But I'm letting you go."*

You didn't have to say forever, because the absence already did.

And so I sat, unmoving, inside the death of us—trying to breathe inside a goodbye I never wanted.

I began talking to you in my head, asking why, begging you to come back, replaying old moments and wondering which one you started slipping away in.

Was it when I cried too much? Held you too tightly? Believed in you more than you believed in yourself? Did I become too much? Or was I never enough?

I clung to our last kiss like it held a secret message I failed to hear the first time. I replayed it so many times, I could taste your goodbye on my tongue before you even said it.

I watched our photos blur—not because of time, but because my eyes refused to stay dry long enough to keep them in focus.

I stopped listening to the songs we used to dance to, they felt like betrayal now, holding hands with memory while mine were empty.

I walked past places we loved and felt haunted, as if joy itself was something I could no longer trust.

I wanted to call you, just to hear your voice, just to ask how the hell you could walk away while still calling it love.

But I didn't, because I knew you weren't mine to reach anymore. That was the part that cut deepest: not that you left, but that you *chose* to.

And I was left with nothing but echoes and questions and a name that used to mean home.

I tried writing letters I never sent. Burned every one. The smoke didn't carry my grief away, but it gave it form—let it rise.

Some nights, I still check for that green dot. Still wonder if you think of me.

But I know better.

Because when someone truly loves you, they don't just let you go. They don't say, *"maybe not now"* and expect you to wait in the wreckage.

Real love stays. Real love fights.

Real love doesn't sound like goodbye, and maybe one day I'll stop loving you. Maybe one day I'll stop writing you into every page I bleed on.

But not today.

Today, I just miss you. Even in your silence. Even in your absence. Even in the death of us.

And if death is all that's left, I'll keep it. Because even death is still a form of having.

{ Burn Me Clean }

I CRIED UNTIL MY throat collapsed in on itself, until the sobs went silent, and even the silence began to scream.

I cried like dying wasn't a metaphor but a method. Grief slipping into my lungs like smoke with no fire alarm, wrapping its hands around my breath, pulling until all that remained were shallow gasps and fractured prayers to a God I no longer knew how to speak to.

It felt like drowning, but slower.

Like you held me under water, not with your hands, but with your absence.

And I stopped fighting for air. Stopped believing in the surface. Laid there, motionless, staring at a ceiling that never blinked back.

Tears slid from the corners of my eyes quiet, uninvited, endless. My body mourning in its own language, a language that didn't need my permission.

My mother sat beside me, her presence fragile but unwavering.

She looked at me like she'd lost her child not to death, but to something crueler: an invisible funeral, where the body still breathes but the soul has gone missing.

She didn't speak at first. Just studied me—the way one might study shattered glass on the floor: too dangerous to sweep, but too delicate to leave untouched.

Then, in a voice soft as unraveling thread, she asked, "Do you wanna watch your favorite movie? Can I make you something to eat?"

I shook my head—barely.

No words.

Only the tremor of grief lodged so deep I was scared it might tear me open if I tried to speak.

She stayed anyway—silent, still, offering presence, not platitudes. She bore witness to my undoing without trying to sew me back together.

Eventually, she reminded me of life—of class, of books, of obligations. But I was failing at the only test that mattered: holding myself together when everything inside me was unraveling.

"I can't go," I whispered. Even my voice sounded unfamiliar—small, cracked, like it had forgotten how to carry me.

"I know how you feel," she said gently. "But maybe it'll help take your mind off it."

But there was no mind to take it off. Grief had become my skin, my breath, my bloodstream, and no distraction could exile it.

I dragged myself to the shower not to cleanse, but to disappear. To grieve in a place where even water couldn't drown the ache.

I scrubbed.

Harder.

Fierce, frantic.

As if pain could be exorcised through skin. As if I could peel you off of me; your hands, your mouth, your ghost. I didn't stop until I saw red. Until the sting of skin screamed louder than memory.

Then I reached for the softest clothes I owned, ones that once felt like love back when I still believed in it. I put them on like armor.

A shield of nostalgia.

I curled back into bed, breath uneven, heartbeat fractured. My body, a battleground of loneliness no echo dared return from.

And then—she came back. My mom. Quietly. Wordlessly.

She pressed play on my favorite movie and climbed in beside me. She didn't try to fix the wreckage. She just stayed. Held space while I fell apart again.

Everyone tried to comfort me as if words could undo what you did. As if language could ever touch the hollow you left.

I was always the bright one. The laugher. The mood-lifter.

"Smiley," they called me.

But after you, I couldn't find *Smiley* anymore. She was gone; buried beneath silence so heavy the house itself mourned.

My father looked at me, eyes full of helpless love. But he couldn't see the war I was fighting. Couldn't feel the rubble I had to crawl through just to get out of bed. Each breath, lifting stone. Each word, a knife swallowed.

And the worst part? I hated myself for still loving you.

I made myself sick circling questions like vultures: Was I ever enough? How do you stop loving someone who left you for dead?

Eventually, the sobbing ended. Not from healing, from depletion. No more tears. No more screaming.

Just silence.

The kind that presses its palms against your ribs and whispers: *stay still*. I sat in the dark. Phone dead. Music off. No distractions. Just me and the echo chamber of my own mind.

I didn't eat. Didn't sleep. Didn't cry.

Just stared at the wall like it might give me answers you never did.

On the outside, stone. Inside, screaming. And the most pathetic part? I still wanted you, still waited, still hoped you'd reach for the wreckage you left me in.

But you didn't. You never did.

And I just sat there burnt, charred, waiting for rescue from the very fire you started.

My mother tried everything: tea, water, food. Desperate offerings from a woman watching her child fade without leaving the room.

She looked at me like someone watching a heartbeat slow.

My father stepped in firm, frightened, tough love. "Cut it out," he said. "You'll end up in the ER. You're dehydrated."

But I didn't care. Didn't move. Didn't feel human anymore.

I couldn't look in the mirror because the person staring back was a ghost wearing my face. I closed my eyes hoping they wouldn't open again, because sleep meant silence. Sleep meant escape.

And honestly?

I don't know how I'm still here, because for a while, I wasn't. I was rubble. Residue. Ash from a fire that never went out.

And the ash, it clings. Even now, it clings.

{ Ghost of Myself }

I didn't move much, eat much. Or even feel much.

My bed became my entire world.

A dim, fabric-wrapped tomb where I laid like a forgotten statue: still in form, but cracked at the core.

I was a body, not a person. Breathing, but not living.

Grief had unpacked its suitcase and settled into the hollow space where joy used to curl up beside me.

Now, it slept there instead coiled and heavy, an animal guarding its own hunger. Appetite was a rumor, a whisper beneath the waves. Not sharp, not urgent just a faint ache I could silence by staying still long enough.

Even blinking felt like a decision. Even existing felt negotiable.

My mother never left, she stayed beside me like a lighthouse that refused to go dark. Sometimes she said nothing just breathed beside me. Other times, she spoke in quiet strands of hope, like stitching light into the folds of my unraveling mind.

Then one afternoon, her voice pierced the fog not loud, but clear, like the first bird you hear after the storm ends, but before the sky believes it.

"Wanna go to the mall?" She smiled. "I'll buy you anything you want."

It wasn't a rescue. It wasn't pressure. It was a reach.

And somehow, God, somehow...I reached back.

I nodded.

A twitch of a smile ghosted my face. Not joy, but something, something small. Something breathing.

I didn't dress up or do my hair. Just sweatpants and a sweatshirt not fashion, but protection. Cotton armor. Soft. Survivable.

We wandered through the mall. My old favorites. Windows I used to press dreams against. Racks filled with pieces of who I used to be.

Before you, fashion was how I screamed: I'm alive. I matter. I shine. A new shirt was a rebirth. A bold jacket was war paint.

But now—I drifted between hangers like a ghost inside a memory.

Nothing fit.

Not my style. Not my skin. Not even the reflection I caught in passing mirrors.

I couldn't find myself in anything.

Couldn't even remember who "myself" was. Just fragments—shards scattered across the tile floor. Pieces of the girl who used to twirl in fitting rooms, who once believed in love, before she drowned in it.

My mom was trying. Held shirts up to me. Offered soft smiles. Believed in a future I could no longer imagine.

"Try it on, it looks good."
"Get that. I'll buy it."

I nodded. I followed. But inside, I was still a vacant room.

We sat to eat, chicken teriyaki, fried dumplings. One of my favorites. I hadn't tasted real food in weeks. She ordered a plate for us to share. I took a few bites not from hunger, but to send a signal: *I'm still trying. Don't give up on me.*

It tasted like memory. Warmth I couldn't hold onto.

And still, I couldn't finish it.

Then we stopped at Diesel. She remembered a belt I once loved, the kind of beautiful, useless thing you never ask for but always dream of.

She bought it—no questions, no lecture. Just love, in the shape of leather and silver. I held it in the bag. The old version of me in my lap.

You would've screamed. You would've posed. You would've captioned it with glitter.

But I just sat there. The belt didn't hold anything together. I was still undone.

When we got home, my dad was waiting. He hugged me like only dads can—not fragile, not soft, but like he was trying to pull me back into the world with the sheer weight of his arms.

"Let's play a funny game," he said—*Cards Against Humanity*. Our thing. He made us drinks. We sat in the living room, and for a moment, laughter waited.

Then it came.

Not forced. Not empty. But real. The ugly-face, stomach-aching kind that breaks open something inside you and lets the air back in.

It didn't save me, didn't erase anything. But it cracked the silence. And for the first time in forever, I felt the echo of someone I used to be.

But that night, the fog returned as it always does. Heavy. Familiar. Seeping beneath the doorframe of my mind.

Both my parents offered to stay up. To watch something, to sit with me inside the ache. I told them no. "I'm tired. I'm gonna go to bed."

So they hugged me one on each side, holding me in place like bookends for a story still being written.

"I had fun with you today," my mom said, hope leaking into the cracks. "You're gonna be okay."

And I broke, again—because I wasn't, and I didn't believe I ever would be.

But that day mattered.

It didn't rescue me. Didn't rewrite the grief. But it reminded me: I am still here. Even if joy feels foreign. Even if nothing fits. Even if I don't recognize the girl in the mirror.

I am still here.

And for now, somehow—that's enough.

{ Florida Knives }

I WAS LEARNING HOW to breathe without your shadow lodged in my lungs. Each inhale a trespass against the graveyard you left behind.

I was relearning survival, how to stand without splintering, how to brush my teeth without tasting shipwreck salt, how to live without bargaining with dawn to turn back time.

I was trying, God, I was clawing at the hours. The days were made of glass. Every second sharp enough to draw blood.

I kept my ribs from collapsing with shaking hands, stitched my own chest shut with thread only I could see, forced my pulse to keep knocking even when my soul begged for silence.

Then one morning no sobbing, no vertigo under my sternum. Not happy. Not whole.

But still.

Still enough to whisper to myself: Maybe. Maybe I'm crawling out. Maybe the worst storm has passed. But grief isn't a storm, it's a predator. It waits. It watches. And when it comes, it doesn't roar, It flickers,

A vibration, A ping. A soft chiming dagger from the pocket I should have left buried.

Your name lit my screen like a flare over enemy territory. Your face. Your sun-drenched laugh.

The Florida sky poured molten gold down your throat like heartbreak had never been invented.

You moved like you had never been hunted. You laughed like my name had never haunted your bones.

And then—the photograph. You and Aria...A kiss, a caption.

"Aria and I are together now."

Aria—the "like a sister" friend. The one you swore was untouchable. The one I was too "insecure" to question. The one you promised you would never cross for the sake of who she was.

Your voice had said, "I would never do that."

But your mouth, the same mouth that once pressed eternity into my ribs was now on Aria's.

It wasn't just the blade.

It was the slow turn of it inside me. It was the grind against bone. You had given your tenderness to another, and I was made to watch.

The carousel spun faster—videos, more kisses, laughter spilling like champagne over my still-open wounds.

Your friends lifted you high, celebrating you like the war had never happened, like you hadn't left landmines buried in my chest.

Palm trees. Pastel skies. Perfectly posed cruelty.

And me, in a dark bedroom drowning in a thousand resurrections of the same day.

No tears at first.

Shock welded my tear ducts shut. I clutched my chest, right where your name used to live.

I opened my mouth to scream but grief sealed my throat in ice.

How could you, Bella?

How could someone who once held my hand like it was the last thread keeping her alive broadcast her detachment like an art piece? How could you feed my fears, call them irrational, and then crown them truth with a kiss?

Like I hadn't kissed your nightmares into submission. Like I hadn't cried into your smile. Like I wasn't the one who stayed when every exit sign screamed at me to run.

You made moving on look cinematic while my healing still reeked of smoke and ash. The world applauded your rebirth, while I was left choking on our corpse.

I didn't know recovery could be ripped out of you in a single frame.

But it can, God, it can...

Because grief writes in volumes. Some chapters whisper. Some howl.

But this one—this one split me open and left me hollow.

I needed to go. Not far, just somewhere that wasn't here.

Somewhere my chest didn't tighten every time your name passed through a room, that name like a warning label I kept trying to peel off with shaking hands never realizing the glue was made to burn.

So I packed light, not enough to weigh me down.

Enough to leave behind the anchors you left me chained to: what you did, what you never apologized for, and the silences you buried me in like shallow graves.

Four hours.

No one spoke, but the silence wasn't empty; it was thick, like air in a sealed room. It pressed against me, and for the first time in months, it didn't feel like it wanted to kill me.

I sat in the backseat, headphones in, music soft, and for once my thoughts weren't screaming. They just...stopped.

Still.

My heart wasn't begging to be understood. It was just beating, steady, mechanical, alive in a way that felt foreign.

I watched the trees smear past the glass, their bodies bending and vanishing, teaching me how to let go without warning.

We arrived.

Cape May—bright, loud, alive. Summer in full swing. I've always hated summer, too loud, too open, like the sun itself is prying. But I went. For the sake of trying. For the sake of not letting the rot win.

We changed, headed for the boardwalk, stopped at a diner frozen in the '80s. The kind of place where time doesn't move, where you could be anyone, even someone who hadn't been gutted. It felt good.

My voice didn't falter. Didn't trip over your name. It was mine again, and whole.

We walked. Laughed. Stopped for pictures. First glance: happy. Second: glassy eyes, fatigue that no nap could touch. Soul-tired, and I hated that it still leaked through the cracks.

Shops—records, rings, vintage shirts. I found one ring, bold, a little too big, heavy like something meant to hold you in place. It looked like strength, so I wore it.

Somehow, I felt less like prey.

We smoked, played glow-in-the-dark mini golf, laughter spilling over nothing and everything. For once my heart wasn't a crime scene.

I blew on water ice like it was soup—a stupid mistake, but we lost it laughing. I didn't care how I looked. Didn't care what you'd think.

For the first time, I simply existed. I had won a stuffed elephant from a coin toss. Gave it to my friend, took a picture, captioned: "I won her an elephant."

Small. Simple. Harmless.

Later, we clinked glasses at a beach bar. Firelight flickered against my skin, soft, forgiving. It felt like a night I used to pray for—the kind you're scared to believe is real.

But peace never lasts. Not when someone refuses to let you have it.

Back at the hotel, lying in bed, music low, scrolling without aim I saw them. Unread messages, stacked one after another.

Your name. Your words. Your damage. Screenshots. The elephant. The drinks. The caption.

"What the hell is this?"
"Clearly, I was never the only one."

I froze.

Your bitmoji staring at me like it had been waiting. Like it never left, like it had been watching.

My heart didn't shatter. It dropped—the way something falls when it knows it's going to break on impact.

I never cheated, I typed. *I'm on vacation with my friends.* Because that's all it was, a vacation.

From you. From the chaos. From the rot.

And yet, anger curled up in my chest, because when you kissed your best friend, I stayed silent. I didn't weaponize my pain. Didn't ruin your peace.

I let you be happy, even if it meant drowning quietly.

Your reply: "I'm not in a good place right now. I'm not stable, and seeing things like this makes it so much harder for me."

That's when it hit me: you never once asked if I was okay.

Not once.

You only demanded my pain as proof, proof I was still loyal, still hurting, still bleeding for you.

And before sleep could take me, I stared at the ceiling, darkness pressing down like an interrogation light, and I whispered to no one: "Why do I always have to be the bigger person?"

Midnight.

The world outside had gone still but inside my chest, a war kept waging, and I was losing.

We were still talking. My thumbs trembled. My heart screamed. My eyes were dry not from healing, but from running out of tears to offer someone who never caught them, only watched them fall like evidence.

Between your messages, I toggled apps like lifelines, scrolling just to feel the ground under me.

Speaking felt dangerous. Louder than my pain. I didn't want to wake my friends, didn't want them to see how fractured I still was beneath the mask I'd welded to my face.

Then—a photo. Your photo.

Red eyes. Tear-streaked cheeks, like a portrait of regret posed for someone else's gallery, and beneath it: "She's already with someone else."

Another punch. Another blade not just stabbed, but twisted. This wasn't grief, this was performance. A funeral you threw for our love and only invited strangers to witness.

I messaged you, "Take it down."

I didn't owe you a thing. But still, I explained myself again. My truth, spilled in lowercase, offered on a platter you never deserved but always took.

I told you: this was my escape. My way of breathing, my way of forgetting. You said you understood. Apologized—for how I felt, not for what you did.

And isn't that worse? The refusal to acknowledge the wound, while still watching it bleed?

I confronted you. Let the one question that's lived inside my ribs like shrapnel since the breakup finally fall from my fingertips: "Are you trying to hurt me again?"

Your reply came fast. Too fast. "What do you mean?"

I stared at the screen, heart pounding like it wanted out, like it knew it was trapped. "It's quite upsetting," I typed, "seeing you kiss your best friend a week after we broke up. You think that didn't affect me?"

And then, the line. The one that made my spine go still: "I was just on a birthday trip with friends. Why is that a problem?"

And suddenly, the quiet inside me wasn't peace—it was fury. Not the loud kind, the cold kind.

The calculated kind.

The kind that watches someone set fire to your home and then ask why you're crying over ash.

"What do you mean...you didn't think that would hurt me?" I wasn't begging for an apology. I just wanted you to see that I bled while you laughed. That I was erased while you rewrote the story without me—a new ending over my unburied body.

But somehow, I found myself calming you down again. Soothing the very hand that struck me. The hand still warm from the match it lit.

Morning came, we went to the beach. It was supposed to be healing. Warm. Soft. Holy. The kind of place that's meant to rinse you clean.

I laid in the shade, towel draped over my face—hiding. Not from the sun, but from the shame. From the weight in my chest that no light could burn away.

AirPods in. Eyes closed. But my mind kept shaking me awake—like a hand on my shoulder in an empty room.

I kept checking my phone, again, and again, for your name, for a sign. For anything that could either save me or drag me back under.

I wasn't falling in love. I was falling back into the pit I had just clawed my way out of. And the pit was smiling, because it knew my shape too well.

I sat up, dissociated, and watched the waves move like clock-work—steady, unbothered, mocking my unrest with their perfect rhythm.

Everyone else was relaxed. Skin warmed. Bodies loose. And I'd never felt more wound tight in my life.

A drink in my hand, salt in my throat. The ocean in front of me. But it wasn't you I was trying to escape anymore.

It was me.

The version of me you left behind—still pacing inside my ribcage.

And somehow, somehow...I was right back where I started. And deep down, in that hollow place I keep pretending I don't feel anymore, I knew it.

You weren't done yet, and neither was the damage.

This was supposed to be my escape. A warm retreat from the wreckage of you. And yet, there I was, on borrowed sand, carrying your name in every breath like a ghost that wouldn't loosen its grip.

Ironic, isn't it?

How you can drive miles from someone, cross oceans of asphalt and air, and still not move an inch inside.

The next day was worse. Not louder. Just heavier. The grief didn't knock. It barged in, flooding the hollow places like it had been waiting to find me again.

We went to dinner. A place that shimmered against the edge of the water, where laughter floated like music and strangers smiled in slow motion. It was golden, alive, the kind of warmth that should feel like comfort. But all I felt was the ache.

I stood in line, surrounded by the scent of grilled something and cheap summer wine, and I thought what I would give to be here with you. To split a meal, to sip from your glass, to look at the view and feel anything but this.

Instead, I swallowed grief like it was oxygen. Choked on it while keeping my face still. No one noticed I was drowning.

After the meal, someone asked, "Boardwalk or shops?"

All I could manage was "I just want to go home."

They didn't ask why. Just looked at me, quiet frowns, soft eyes and said, "Okay. Let's go." Back at the hotel, we packed. I took the backseat.

There's something sacred about hiding behind someone else's shoulders when you're unraveling quietly.

I put on my headphones. Noise canceling. Closed my eyes and let my head lean to the side, resting on a rolled towel like a child faking sleep. But I was awake.

So painfully awake.

They thought I was resting. But I was replaying every mile, every memory, watching you walk through the corridors of my mind as the highway unfolded in shadows.

Four hours. Four hours of being nowhere except in your orbit.

We got home at 11 p.m.

I walked in like a ghost haunted by my own reflection. Straight to the bathroom. Dropped my bag, undressed, and there in the mirror, was the version of me I didn't recognize anymore.

Swollen eyes. Hollowed cheeks. Ribs sharp and visible, like they were trying to claw their way through skin just to escape the weight of my chest. A face that had forgotten how to look like love.

My body?

Collapsed scaffolding. Starved of more than food.

The weight I'd lost, twenty pounds—wasn't an accident. It was muscle memory erased, flesh surrendered. Evidence that something inside me had been gnawed away until there was nothing left to protect.

I stepped into the shower, turned the heat all the way up. Let it scald. Let it bite. The sting began at my calves, raw from the sun, angry red from carelessness. No sunscreen. No protection. I hadn't cared to save myself. And then I turned, just slightly, and the water found the scars.

I froze.

The steam curled around me, the sound of water filling the silence as my mind slipped backwards to the night I stopped pretending I was strong.

Red was your favorite color. I remember thinking that as I carved your name into my body. Watched the blood drip to the floor, pooling like it had somewhere better to be.

The memory evaporated, but the chill it left behind didn't. I was still standing there, motionless under the heat, the water running down my face.

My lips parted just enough to whisper to no one, *I hope red is still your favorite color.*

The water didn't heal. Not this time. Even the thing meant to soothe burned me.

Everything hurt. Inside. Outside. Like my body had joined in on the mourning my soul had already begun.

I stepped out, pulled on soft clothes like armor. Didn't dry my hair. Didn't look back. Just crawled into bed a wet, heavy thing sinking into cold sheets like the earth had opened up to take me whole.

Sleep didn't come, because pain this loud doesn't whisper.

It howls.

It plays lullabies in the form of memories, it rocks you with the same hands that once cradled your joy.

And in the dark, under the hum of the fan and the pulse in my ears, I realized something I had been avoiding far too long: you hadn't just broken my heart, you convinced me I was the one holding the hammer.

...And that's how you win, isn't it? You hurt me, then hand me the blame like it's a gift. You made me bleed and still convinced me the knife was mine.

But here's the truth: I was never the weapon. I was the target. I was the offering.

And you?

You were always the one swinging.

{ Too Sharp to Love }

THE TRUTH CUT DEEPER: your friends were not innocent by-standers. They wore blindfolds to my suffering: silk ribbons tied tight over their eyes, choosing darkness over the sight of me breaking. They stood inches from the wreckage, close enough to feel the heat of it, but refused to see.

I could hear the quiet shuffle of their feet, the way people move when they know they're stepping around something sharp.

And in that instant, it wasn't just about you anymore.

It was every time I'd been invisible. Every time my pain went unacknowledged. Every time I had to convince the world I was worth saving.

I remember thinking: Do I want love, or do I just want to prove that I'm lovable?

Not the kind of love that's easy, not the kind that arrives wrapped in ribbon. But the kind that is willing to crawl through glass, to bleed a little, to hold me anyway.

Proof that someone could take whatever mess was left of me and not recoil. The mess wasn't abstract—it was shattered glass.

Jagged edges glittering across the floor of my childhood bedroom.

I can still see the way the morning light would hit them, little knives of sunlight thrown across the carpet.

No one dared to step inside. No one wanted to touch me. No one wanted to hold me. They were afraid they'd bleed.

Funny thing about glass: people only call it dangerous when it's in your hands. Nobody warns you about the ones who drop it. Nobody tells you how their silence cuts deeper than any shard you could ever carry.

And now, here I am again, years later, different heartbreak, same lesson.

The moment the truth came out, and your friends chose to look away, I felt the confirmation in my bones. A verdict delivered without a single word: They wouldn't save me. They wouldn't even see me.

It was the same silence I grew up with. The same cold refusal to reach for me.

The same turning of heads, as if my pain was contagious. The same unspoken verdict: You are too sharp to love.

And that truth burned hotter than any rage I've ever known. It was not the kind of fury that rips the air apart.

It was the kind that sits with you in the dark, like a shadow pressed to your skin, whispering that you will have to save yourself.

Am I too sharp to love?

No.

They were too fragile to touch me. That's the truth no one ever says out loud. It's easier for them if the blame lives in my body, if the glass is my fault, not theirs.

But listen—glass doesn't cut until someone drops it. They dropped me. They looked away. They decided I wasn't worth the reach.

Me?

I was never the weapon. I was always proof of how weak they are.

I am not too sharp to love. I am sharp because you broke me, and still, I shine.

{ The White Sheet }

You left me.

Not with words. Not with truth.

You left me with the dignity of not understanding, and maybe that was the cruelest part.

You walked away holding the story, I stayed behind, clutching the ache, a wound I couldn't stitch.

You smiled for your feed. I screamed into pillows.

I tried to glue myself back together with trembling hands, with unanswered texts.

The pieces...they never fit. They sliced me open again, and again.

Tell me...was I just your burden? Was my love too loud for your curated silence?

Did you call it *"mental health"* when what you really meant was: *"Freedom. Relief. Escape."*

Why was loving me the first thing to go? Too real in a world where you wanted to float? Did I remind you of everything you were desperate to outrun?

Because it didn't look like pain in your story. When you laughed, when you kissed, when you performed your freedom for strangers.

While I...

I sat in the dark. Hands shaking, trying to hold the weight of an earthquake.

Tell me the truth—was I just your soft escape?

A clean white sheet you could drape over the blood on my hands—my hands, blood from trying to hold something already slipping through my fingers.

You could have said it. "I don't love you anymore."

But no.

Instead, you chose: "I'm not okay, mentally."

And I softened, I believed you. I cradled those words, like they might shatter in my hands.

But then...You went on.

Laughter sharp enough to cut through my chest. Photos glowing as if grief had never brushed your skin. No shadows where you claimed darkness lived.

And me?

I was drowning in your absence.

The silence that crawls under your skin, that burrows in. The silence that whispers: You were disposable.

If you weren't okay...why did it cost us everything?

This wasn't kindness. This wasn't honesty. This wasn't care.

It was abandonment wearing a soft mask. A sugarcoated blade.

And it cut...just the same.

So I wonder...was there never a storm at all? Just a convenient cloud...A hiding place for you to vanish while I waited at the window.

You stopped showing up. In body, in heart, in spirit, but lingered just enough...A like on my story.

A heart on a meme.

Tiny sparks thrown into darkness...Enough to keep me standing at the edge.

You kept my heart on a leash. Tight enough to remind me it was yours. Loose enough for you to wander, because how do you walk away from someone you love?

You don't.

And deep down...I think you always knew I wouldn't.

That's why you dangled the leash. That's why you slipped the knife so quietly between my ribs. You knew I'd stand there bleeding, hands shaking, still begging to hold the weight of an earthquake...while you built a new life on steadier ground.

You called it freedom. You called it healing.

But really...It was me unraveling in silence, while you walked away smiling. Never once turning back to watch me fall.

Now, all I see...Is a demon in the shape of the girl I loved.

Something that once felt like home now haunts the corners of my nightmares.

You don't have to speak. Your memory does the damage.

And the worst part? I'd still go back...if I thought there was a sliver of you that remembered how you loved me.

That's how broken I am, still reaching for the hands that pushed me into the fire.

{ 'Til Sleep Do Us Part }

BEFORE THE FIRST WORD between us, you undid me.

You cleaved my life in two: before you, and after you, and I have never wished to live in the first half again.

Bella, I vow to carry you through days too heavy for either of us to bear alone.

To steady you when the ground turns unkind. To release you when your dreams grow wings.

I vow to memorize the map of you, the way your laughter breaks the light, the crease at your mouth when you fight a smile, the way you leaned into me as though my body were the only shelter you trusted.

I vow to love you not only in brightness but in the unlit corridors where the silence presses like stone. I vow to build a cathedral vast enough to hold both your light and your shadows.

And when life ends, when the veil falls and the world forgets us, I'll search the dark until I find you.

Even if the earth must be crossed on broken knees. Even if the heavens have no door. Even if all that remains of me is a whisper in the marrow of time.

If there is a forever, Bella, it wears your name.

We stand at the altar. I kiss you as the night we first met—gentle, and yet enough to set the world alight. One hand on your cheek, the other at your back, holding you as though I could never let go.

Here, in my dream, at the afterparty, I call you to the piano. You rise and come to me.

I guide you to sit on the instrument; your dress brushes the polished wood, your eyes fixed on mine.

I begin to play.

The first key, *A Thousand Years*—and you know the song at once. Your gaze softens; tears catch light. This is it, I think, this is what love looks like.

The room glows safe and golden. Then something shifts. A draft whispers through the hall though no doors open. The chandelier trembles above us.

My fingers hesitate, stumble on a note yet the melody continues as though the piano no longer needs me.

The keys press themselves down. Ivory clicking in a rhythm I do not command. The harmony fractures. Sweetness bends sharp, chords spilling like broken glass. The song becomes a dirge, every note heavier than bone.

I try to stop. I try to lift my hands. But they are fastened to the keys as if unseen strings pull them into motion.

I look at you. Your smile splits too wide, cutting across your face like a wound. Your eyes sink hollow, black wells that catch no light.

Blood slicks down the polished wood, seeping between the keys, dripping onto the floor in dark rivulets.

Where your hand should rest is something else- scaled, clawed, scratching deep furrows into the piano's surface.

The air thickens. Metallic. A furnace of iron and smoke coils around us.

I choke.

I know, suddenly, I am not playing for you. It isn't you.

It never was.

The demon tilts its head, wearing your face like a mask too tight for its bones. A grin splits into too many teeth.

It leans toward me, whispering in your stolen voice: *I wear her face because you gave it to me.*

The words hook beneath my skin, dragging, my vows shrivel to ash.

The cathedral of my love crumbles stone by stone. Still the hymn pours on, a ruin I cannot silence.

And then, silence.

The dream is gone, yet the cold remains. The air in my room is sharp, emptied of warmth.

A hand strokes my cheek. Tender. Familiar.

I gasp awake. My eyes are open.

The demon sits at the edge of my bed, caressing me, smiling. I do not scream, the sound lodges in my chest, strangled, as though the dream still has me by the throat. My skin burns where it touched me, though the room is cold enough to make my breath fog.

For a moment, I cannot tell if my eyes are open, if this is waking at all, or just another dream layered on the first.

I turn on the lamp. The room stares back—bare walls and quiet shadows. Nothing sits at the edge of my bed, yet the indentation in the blanket remains, a hollow pressed deep as if someone has only just risen.

I press my palms to my face, trembling.

My vows echo in my skull, broken fragments; *I vow to steady you. I vow to love you in the unlit corridors.*

But what if I built those vows for a ghost? What if I opened a cathedral only to let a demon in?

Sleep won't return. I rise. Pace my bedroom's floor. Touch every corner of the room to prove it is still mine.

And still, I cannot shake the chill, the certainty that something has crossed the threshold.

When dawn comes, I will write it down. Every word. Every shadow. Because if I don't, I fear the dream will keep rewriting itself until I no longer know which face is yours, and which is the thing that smiled at me in the dark.

...I wanted to call your name. To feel you in the waking world.

But what if I call...and only hear the demon laughing back?

{ Paper Ghosts }

Bella, you're still here. Aren't you?

Not in flesh. Not in blood. No, you're sharper than that.

You prefer the quiet places. The corners where light doesn't reach. The walls that creak when no one's moving.

You linger in every silence that knows my name, and maybe that's the cruelest trick of all: you're gone, but you never really leave. You trail me like a paper ghost, thin enough to slip through cracks, heavy enough to press the air from my lungs.

I tell myself it's memory, tell myself it's grief, but deep down, I know better. You're watching. You always were.

Perhaps, the hardest part is never the sound of a door closing. It isn't the rupture itself, nor the silence that follows like a shadow settling into bone.

It is the long unraveling, the day you recognize, with reluctant grace, that the soul you once loved without condition must be released.

Not because the love has vanished, but because the lives you are meant to lead no longer walk the same road.

I wish I had reached that wisdom whole. But I didn't.

I broke first.

Splintered long before my hands could unclench. The memory drifts through me still, blurred like film left too long in the sun: colors dulled, edges bleeding into shadow, a fragile world already half-lost.

I've watched. Always.

The new life you've built, carefully polished, glowing for the world to admire, you think it hides you.

It doesn't. It never has.

Shadows do not respect calendars.

They wait. They learn. They follow. They study habits, and they never forget.

I know your rhythm, Bella.

Every laugh you reserve for strangers. Every glance you think is unobserved. Every breath you take that you believe is your own. I know, and I never stop knowing.

You float through your days, untouchable, thinking time can bury me.

You think freedom has saved you. But shadows do not disappear.

Not for you. Not for me, and certainly not for the one who remembers everything.

You think you escaped it. You think I escaped it. But I'm not bound by sleep or memory.

I follow the echoes.

I follow the softest sound you make, the small movements no one else notices.

You think you've hidden yourself in light. But the shadows remember.

I know where you go, Bella. I know what you leave behind. I know the spaces you think are empty. I know the people who touch you. I know the smiles that are not mine.

Time cannot save you. Distance cannot save you. Memory cannot save you.

You can scrub the past clean. You can drape your life in light. But I am in the shadows.

I am in the walls. I am in the air you breathe.

I am in the part of you that remembers me, even when you tell yourself I am gone.

And when you finally look over your shoulder, don't be surprised when I'm the one smiling back.

{ The Truth I Keep }

You walked away first.

And yet...you still try to hold the reins of my voice. Still try to decide how I remember the wounds you left.

You call me a hypocrite for caring.

My book isn't proof I never loved you, it's proof that I did.

If I hadn't cared, there would be no knife. No blood. No story.

The words I write now...They are scars.

You drove the blade into my chest. Watched me gasp, drown in the red silence you made.

And you? You walked away. Never once looking back.

I clawed at the knife lodged in my ribs. Fingers slipping on the handle, slick with my own blood.

It wasn't a pull. It was a slow extraction. A sound like fabric tearing inside me.

Each inch of steel dragged out a shudder, a gasp, a prayer I didn't believe in anymore.

I lifted it into the light. The blade caught my reflection, a stranger's eyes staring back. And then, somehow, I stood on trembling legs, chest split open but empty of your weapon.

Call me the villain if you must. Paint me in darkness if it keeps your conscience clean. We both know the truth.

You struck first.

I survived.

You rewrote my survival as violence. You painted my healing as harm.

But I know the truth. You wounded me.

If my blood stains your story, it's only because you refused to stop cutting.

I am not your harbor for anxieties. I am a locked room. Lights off.

And you?

You yell through the crack in the door. Your accusations roll off me like rain on glass.

They cling to you.

Silence is not empty. Silence accumulates weight. It remembers.

I could name you in a paragraph. I could hand you the proof you crave. But I won't.

Charity is not on my ledger.

Keep your messages.

Buzz like flies against a closed window. Small. Frantic. Certain the world owes you.

You want to know what this says about me? It says I learned to preserve myself. It says I owe no one a story but my own.

You call me uncaring. You're right. Care was a currency I spent when I thought you were worth the cost.

You don't get to play both the executioner and victim. You lost the right to my narrative the day you chose betrayal over love.

Now you're worried if you're painted in a bad light? Darling, you did that yourself. You did it all yourself.

I used to think you were a good person. I thought trauma had touched you, not broken you. What did I know?

Now I see.

You are terrible. You are a terrible person and you destroyed my heart.

You are the reason I flinch at love now—congratulations. You made your scar deep within me. You did a terrible thing.

Not a mistake. Not a lapse.

A choice. A betrayal.

Turns out, I was loving a beautifully constructed lie all along.

I embraced every version of you, Bella, even the ones broken by hands that came before mine. I reached for your pain with open palms, hoping you'd feel safe in my care, but I ended up covered in blood, cut by the very pieces I tried to hold together.

Now, every time someone says the word *love,* something inside me recoils. My body doesn't recognize it as something safe anymore. It flinches—like its heard a gunshot instead of a word meant to heal.

I try to speak of it, but my voice betrays me, shaky, uneven, like a violin string stretched too tight.

I always believed love was soft, that it could be a place to rest, a home I could build inside someone's chest.

But you, Bella, took that belief and dismantled it slowly—not all at once, but piece by piece until the foundation crumbled while I was still decorating the walls.

Now, I speak of love like its a ghost story. Not because its dead, but because it haunts me.

I don't fear being alone, I fear loving again and not knowing if I'll survive it next time, and maybe that's the deepest bruise you left:

not just that you broke my heart, but that you made me question whether love was real to begin with.

For anyone reading this, let my story place a gentle hand on your shoulder. Let it warn you in the quiet way pain sometimes does.

Don't make the mistake I made. Don't let hope blind you.

People can be beautiful on the surface, and dangerous in the shadows.

They can smile as they undo you. They can love you with hands that were never meant to hold you.

Save yourself the unraveling.

Listen to the small voice inside you—the one that trembles before you do. Trust the red flags when they whisper instead of scream.

As for me?

I gathered my broken pieces with trembling fingers. I stitched myself back together in the long, quiet hours of my healing.

Don't think for a second that silence is weakness. Because silence remembers, and it waits, and sometimes, if you listen closely...it smiles.

Perhaps this is how our journey was always meant to end.

Maybe this was the universe's way of teaching me how to finally let go.

Because, Bella...if you hadn't said those words, those sharp, careless words, that cut deeper than you realized, I would still be here. I would never have walked away from someone who once meant so much to me.

But you pushed me.

You pushed me with your silence, with your indifference, with the way you tossed my heart aside as though it had never been worth holding.

Don't worry, Bella. You're free now.

You don't have to carry me anymore—I've already lifted myself from the place you kept pushing me out of.

The grave you dug for our love will only hold you. I will not climb down there. I will not bury myself beside something that died at your hands.

So I leave you, with the shovel, with the dirt under your nails, with the ghost of what we almost became.

I STAND AT THE edge of that grave.

The earth is damp.

Cold air carries the echo of everything unsaid.

In my hands,

a bouquet of roses. Once red.

Now blackened and brittle.

Their thorns dulled,

their petals curled inward like secrets.

I kneel.

Set the dead bouquet at the base of the stone.

My fingers linger on the stems,

one last tremor of goodbye.

And as I rise,

as I turn to leave, I lean in close.

My breath, a ghost in the cold air. "Flowers for you, my love."

Then silence.

Only silence.

And me, walking away.

About the Author

Lyss Agri is an author and entrepreneur from New York whose work explores the thin line between passion and pain, love and loss. Their writing sits in the moments that bruise and illuminate—the places where beauty and devastation coexist, where desire burns even as it comes undone.

Their debut novel, *Six Months of Forever*, is a sapphic dark romance that examines the haunting beauty of impermanent love and the price of opening one's heart. It traces what happens when love feels fated yet never secure, and how the things that break us can also remind us we are still alive.

Drawn to the intricacies of human emotion, Lyss writes characters who are magnetic, flawed, and achingly real. Through their work, they invite readers to face the raw truths of intimacy: that love can steady us, undo us, and sometimes do both in the same breath.

You can find Lyss on Instagram at @vigilanci_.